—•••—

INTERCEPT

A Treacherous Race
to the Triple Crown

—•••—

House of Beads Mystery Series, Book 2

MARY JANE FORBES

Todd Book Publications

INTERCEPT

A Treacherous Race to the Triple Crown

ISBN: 978-0615954769 (sc)
Printed in the United States of America
Todd Book Publications, 2nd Edition: 7/2010
4th Edition: 10/2017
Port Orange Florida

Website: www.MaryJaneForbes.com
Author photo: Ami Ringeisen

Acknowledgements

Thanks to my family—my daughter, Molly; my brother-in-law, Dick; and my nephew's wife, Corby—for reading the initial draft. Your feedback helped enormously.

Joey Stevens—thank you for your insight to the everyday struggles and bravery of an amputee.

Thank you to Senior Chief Boatswain's Mate, Newman Cantrell, Jr. for information about the New Smyrna Beach Coast Guard Station.

Thanks to the NSERB (North Side Editorial Review Board) Vera, Lorna, Jean, and Adele, as well as Roger and Pat Grady, and Geri Rogers for struggling through the initial draft.

Ami Ringeisen—thanks for taking the author's photo.

Thanks to Adele Brinkley for her initial editing.

My acknowledgements would not be complete without mentioning the bead shop, Imagine That!®, where the House of Beads Mystery Series began. Carolyn and Scott—thank you for your continued support.

—•••—

INTERCEPT is the second book in a series of four. Look for book three, CHECKMATE, in a few months. In the meantime, find a comfy chair and enjoy the following pages as Hutch, Catherine, Manny, and Peaches struggle to find and apprehend the bad guys.

Please visit my website:

www.MaryJaneForbes.com

–•••–

Intercept

–•••–

Chapter 1

— • • • —

"MAYDAY! MAYDAY!" The distress call crackled the ham radio to life.

Ocean waves beat the shores of Florida. Hurricane force winds picked up torrential rain slamming the drops like thousands of pellets against the glass of the high-rise condo. Relentless, the tropical storm raged on.

Hearing the call for help over his radio, Pete grabbed his binoculars training them on the raging ocean, but he couldn't see through the sheets of rain. The NOAA weather station broadcasting non-stop warnings of the powerful storm that had been pounding Daytona Beach for over an hour. Anybody out in this weather was suicidal.

The ham radio crackled again. Flinging the binoculars onto the couch, Pete spun his wheelchair around snatching the ham radio's mouthpiece from its hook.

"Daytona Pete responding to mayday call. I hear you out there. What are your coordinates? Who are you? Over," Pete said, speaking calmly into the receiver. His voice was calm, but his hand shook. Pete heard a faint crackle emanate from the radio, but he couldn't make out the words. He moved closer, bent his head down, concentrating to decipher the words, his hair touching the fine mesh of the speaker.

"John Anderson, skipper..." shouted the distorted voice.

"Anderson, you're breaking up. Please repeat, where are you? Over."

"John Anderson, skipper of the Molly C. We ran out of fuel trying to escape the storm. Over."

"I hear you, Molly C. What is your location? Over."

"We're approaching Ponce Inlet lighthouse. We're taking on water...tossed around...over."

"Gotcha, Molly C. I'll call the coast guard. Hang on. Out."

Pete quickly dialed his friend Chuck Colton, Captain, U.S. Coast Guard, New Smyrna Beach. "Chuck, I received a mayday call minutes ago over my ham radio. The skipper said he was approaching Ponce Inlet lighthouse. His name is John Anderson. The boat is the Molly C. He has no fuel and is taking on water."

"Thanks, Pete. Hang on a minute. Let me check with my Officer of the Day."

Pete nervously waited for Chuck to come back on the line. Startled, he dropped the phone into his lap when a large frond from a nearby palm hit his balcony window sending a loud crashing sound through his living room. He quickly retrieved the receiver.

"Pete. Pete, are you there?" Colton called out to him.

"Yep, I'm here. What did you find out?"

"We received the mayday call. My officer notified the Savannah, Georgia, Air Station. They will dispatch a chopper as soon as the weather permits. Unfortunately, it doesn't look good. We'll send a boat out as soon as we can, but as it stands now, it is too risky. Did you receive the call on Channel 16?"

"Yes, I did. Shit, something else just hit my window. I feel like a sitting duck up here in the sky."

"If you pick him up again on any other channel, let me know. You can monitor the progress from your end."

"Copy that." Pete hung up the phone and returned to his ham radio.

"Molly C, Daytona Pete here. The coast guard knows your situation. Choppers are grounded for now. Stay on Channel 16. Over."

Pete received no reply.

"Molly C, Daytona Pete here. Do you read me? Over."

Again no reply.

The silence was punctuated by sporadic crackling from his radio. The storm grew more intense as the ocean waves pounded the shore. The waves carried sand out to sea as they retreated, causing uncontrollable beach erosion. Pete noted the time on his watch; it was 5:30 in the afternoon. The sky appeared dark as charcoal.

Pete punched the redial button on his phone. "Chuck, did you hear from the Molly C again?" he asked.

"No. Savannah is trying to send a chopper up, but the winds are still too strong. Keep in touch."

—•••—

AROUND 2:00 A.M. the next morning, the Coast Guard Station received a reported sighting of a boat off New Smyrna Beach. She was hung up on a sandbar, lolling back and forth. By now, the storm had passed out to sea. All vestiges of the nightmarish weather—howling wind and torrential rain—were gone. Mother Nature had left her mark with sand gullies and debris scattered on the shore by the receding tide.

Pete's phone rang. Picking up the receiver, he saw the sun breach the horizon outside his balcony's sliding glass doors.

"Good morning, Pete," Chuck said. "Your mayday boat was spotted early this morning, and we've checked her out. If you keep this up, Pete, we're going to put you on the payroll."

"No way, I'm having too much fun protecting your back side. Where did you find her, and how is John Anderson?"

"The Molly C is in good shape. She beached herself on the New Smyrna shore. Her hull suffered a few scrapes where she hit some rocks, but nothing that can't be fixed. John Anderson is a different story. He's dead. Shot once in the head."

Chapter 2

— • • • —

AT 7:30 IN THE MORNING, Captain Manny Salinas, Daytona Beach Police Department, Criminal Investigation Division, walked into his office with his dog, Peaches, by his side. The phone was ringing as he approached his desk. He punched the speaker button so he could talk while setting his coffee down and scanning his message slips from the night patrol.

"Hi, Manny, Chuck Colton here."

"You coast guard guys must have been pretty busy yesterday," Manny said. "That was quite a storm that tore through our area. The department was jumping with accidents by idiots driving too fast. Some of them hydroplaned right off the road, but back to you. Somehow, I don't think this is a social call. What's up?"

"You're right. I have a body for you. He's down in New Smyrna Beach—shot in the head. We found him on the aft deck of a beached yacht. His clothes were entangled on one of the cleats. If he hadn't been snagged by the cleat, he would probably have washed overboard. The boat hung up on a sandbar early this morning. We think his name is John Anderson. There was no ID on his body or in the boat."

"What makes you think his name is John Anderson if there was no ID?" Manny asked.

"Do you know Pete Peterson? He's also known as Daytona Pete."

"I've heard of him. Isn't he the Iraq war vet who talks to passing ships from his condo in Daytona Beach Shores?"

"He's the one. He picked up a mayday call on his ham radio at the height of the storm late yesterday afternoon. The caller identified himself as John Anderson. Said he ran out of fuel and was taking on water. We received the same mayday call, but when we tried to contact Anderson, we got nothing but dead air so we notified the Savannah Air Station. They couldn't respond at the time with a chopper because of the weather. The storm intensified, but the station did send a chopper out a little after 3:00 a.m. When the storm passed out to sea, the moon came out. They saw her, the Molly C, beached on a sandbar."

"I'll notify the medical examiner. How do we find her?" Manny asked, taking a sip of his coffee. Peaches was already asleep on her pillow, tired from their morning jog.

"Take Route 1 to New Smyrna Beach. Proceed on the north causeway and Flagler Avenue to the beach access ramp. Drive onto the sand and hook a left. You'll see her up a ways. I have a guy watching her. Just show him your badge. I'll let him know you're coming."

Leaving the speaker connected, Manny put in a call to the department's medical examiner, Sam Houston. "Sam, glad to see you're in early. Giving the taxpayers their money's worth, are you?"

"I dare say probably more than you've given them this morning," Sam replied. "How's my furry friend?"

"Peaches is napping at the moment," Manny said, watching the dog's tail give a thump when she heard her name. "I just received a call from the Coast Guard Station. They found a body on a beached boat. I'll go with you to pick him up. He's still on the vessel in New Smyrna."

"You're lucky. I was just about to start an autopsy. I'll swing by for you in the wagon."

Manny disconnected the call. He slapped his thigh to get the attention of his best friend. "Come on, Peaches. We're going for a little ride."

Peaches, a black Labrador retriever, had been with Manny for two years. They found each other at a farmer's market. She was a stray. Not long into their relationship, Manny witnessed that Peaches displayed some pretty sophisticated training, more than likely military. In one instance, while on a case with Manny, Peaches performed a search and rescue and saved a girl's life. The dog also took down the killer in the same case. After the first nuzzle at the market, she never left Manny's side. He liked to say they adopted each other. The day after the adoption he placed a cedar-filled pillow next to his desk.

From then on, anytime you saw Manny you could bet Peaches was by his side.

By the time Manny and Peaches walked outside, Sam had arrived driving the morgue's wagon. The captain and his dog piled into the vehicle, and Sam headed south for the twenty-five minute drive to the stranded boat. Accessing the beach from the ramp off Flagler Avenue, the three bumped along the ruts and debris in the sand left by the storm. The boat was visible a few yards ahead. She looked like a toy, swaying gently from side to side on the water. The waves, no longer threatening, were not strong enough to free her.

The Coast Guard officer saw them coming and climbed down the rope ladder he had thrown over the stern to facilitate getting on and off the vessel. "Hi. The captain said to expect you. Sorry, the rope ladder is the only way to come aboard."

The men shook hands and introduced themselves. Peaches dashed off, romping through the lapping waves, chasing a flock of sandpipers, having a glorious time. Manny called her back and put her in the wagon until he could see what they were up against.

Until the men climbed the ladder, the body, snared on the cleat, could not be seen because of the angle the boat was listing. The lieutenant boarded first, then Manny. Sam handed him his forensic kit and camera and joined them on board.

There was no blood on the deck. The waves from the night's storm had washed it clean. Manny and Sam pulled on white latex gloves and approached the body.

"I didn't move him, figuring you would want to see how he was entangled," the lieutenant said. "The deck was clean as you can see, but the galley is spattered with blood. I figure he was shot in the galley and then hauled out here to be thrown overboard."

"The poor bastard looks like he's staring at us," Manny said, crouching down beside the corpse. "His face, what's left of it, is scrubbed clean by the waves. Look, Sam, the blood even ran down his pants. He must have been in the galley for more than a few minutes with the amount of blood on his clothes. They were soaked before this cleat snared him and the waves washed over his body." Being a seasoned police officer, Manny had learned over the years to blunt his emotional reactions to a murder scene. Nevertheless, a feeling of sorrow always shot up from the pit of his stomach when he responded to a crime where the victim had met a violent end to his or her life on earth.

Sam nodded in agreement as he opened his forensic kit.

"We'll have to impound the boat," Manny said. "She's fairly large. What would you guess, Lieutenant, forty feet?"

"She's actually forty-four feet. It will take a crane to lift her out of the hole she's created. High tide is at 3:12 this afternoon."

"I'll call Pelican Bay Marina in Daytona Beach," Manny said. "They have the equipment to do the job. Most of their boats are out of storage, so I think they'll be able to cordon off an area for her. Sam, let's do a walk through without disturbing anything. Take whatever pictures you need of the body and then we'll transport him to your lab."

Manny crouched down again at the back of the deck. "Sam, take a look at this piece of rope tied to the rail. It's frayed on the end. Whatever was tied is long gone when the line pulled apart or was severed. When you go back to the wagon bring a brown paper bag, will you? I'm taking this rope back to Dani for analysis."

Manny called the marina making arrangements for the boat to be rescued while Sam took pictures of the body from various angles. Sam climbed down the ladder, walked to the bow of the boat, taking more pictures. Satisfied, he went to the wagon to retrieve a stretcher as well as a body bag and wide belts to secure the victim. Peaches jumped out and ran into the water.

Early-morning joggers were beginning to gather, gawking at the beached boat. They watched Sam and Manny load the body into the wagon with the help of the lieutenant. Sensing the fun was over, Peaches jumped into the vehicle. Sam turned the wagon around, and they headed back to the police department.

"Do you think it's suicide?" Manny asked.

"Not a chance," Sam said, turning right onto Route 1. "The bullet entered near the back of his head. It would be virtually impossible for him to inflict that kind of wound himself. I'd say the case calls for a higher authority than we provide. You have a murder on the high seas, my friend."

"I agree. I'd better notify Agent Hutchinson, Homeland Security," Manny said. "We worked together on the illegal immigrant case last month. Hell, he might as well take up residence down here."

Chapter 3

— • • • —

SAM DROPPED MANNY and peaches off at the department and continued on to the morgue to tend to the body. Before going up to his office, Manny pulled out his cell, retrieved the Homeland Security number and hit Send.

"Agent Hutchinson."

"Hutchinson, this is Captain Salinas."

"Manny, what's with the Captain horseshit?" Hutch said. "It's only been a couple of months since you worked with me."

"I think you assisted me in that case," Manny retorted.

"Whatever." Hutch sighed heavily. "Why are you calling? I'm sure it isn't because you're wondering about my love life."

"I could care less about your personal affairs. Last night a tropical storm blew through here and beached a yacht. A civilian intercepted a mayday call from a man. The yacht was found this morning on the shores of New Smyrna Beach."

"Okay. I ask you again, why are you calling me?"

"A dead man was found on board, shot in the head. Our medical examiner picked up the body. I'm only calling to alert you to the fact that we don't know if he was killed out in the ocean or after the boat was beached. However, it probably happened out at sea and whoever killed him may have been washed overboard."

"I see. I'm working a case right now, but I might be able to break away to see what you've got."

"Oh, you don't have to come down. I'm only alerting you to what happened."

"I don't know what's sticking in your craw, Manny. Please let me know what the coroner finds. I may or may not be down in the next twenty-four hours," Hutch said and hung up.

Manny closed his cell. "Great. Just great. He's probably looking for an excuse to see Catherine again and I served her up on a platter." He swatted his shirt pocket for his Nicorette gum. "Damn habit," he muttered, tearing the wrapper away and jamming the gum into his mouth.

Chapter 4

— • • • —

IT WAS NOW NINE-THIRTY. Manny and Peaches went into the department and headed for the bullpen.

Manny wanted to foster open communication with his team so he designed the area in the shape of an octagon. The area quickly became known as the bullpen. The team could swing their chairs around to face each other and the electronic whiteboards. The case whiteboards took up two sides of the octagon. With the push of a button, the information written, drawn, or scribbled on a board was saved to a computer file. Once the information was saved, the boards could be wiped clean with a special solution ready to be written on again. So far this morning, the boards were clean; a condition that was about to change.

Manny's team consisted of two detectives, Fred Watson and George Anderson, and a sergeant, Dani Trotter.

Detective Fred Watson, thirty-seven, was recruited from Santa Fe, New Mexico. The day Fred decided on a career in law enforcement was the day he went into his bathroom and shaved off his thick, afro-style hair. He had reported to Manny for three years.

Detective George Anderson, twenty-nine, was recruited two years after graduation with a Bachelor of Science, Law Enforcement, from the University of Michigan. After his graduation, he served on a Detroit police squad. His six-foot-one frame appeared thin, but he was strong as an ox. Fred and George were perfect foils for each other.

Sergeant Dani Trotter graduated with a Bachelor of Science degree. She spent five years at West Virginia University to claim the title of forensic scientist. She plays her computer keyboard like a Stradivarius violin. Black-leather cushioned shoes anchor her small frame. She always wears a black turtleneck T-shirt, long-sleeved, because of the morgue-like temperature in her lab. Her black hair, tucked behind her ears, with streaks of blonde framing her face of flawless, porcelain skin. She loves her job and looks at every assignment she's given as a puzzle. Manny recruited her fresh out of college two years ago.

Entering the bullpen, Peaches plopped down on her bed exhausted from her morning romp in the water. The team turned to face Manny as he headed for the case board.

"Glad to see you're all here," Manny said, still chewing hard on his gum. "Last night's storm beached a yacht in New Smyrna. An hour ago, Sam and I transported the body found on the boat to the morgue. Here's what we have so far," he said, speaking as he wrote. "Victim: white male, shot in the head." Manny turned to face the group. "The only reason we have a body is because his clothes became entangled on one of the boat's cleats. Sam will give us a report on John Doe later today. I'd put his age in the forties. Dani, Sam has pictures of the body and the boat. Please get prints and post them beside the board."

Manny went to his desk, picked up his notes, and opened a fresh bottle of ice-cold water. His composure now under control, the cryptic conversation with Hutch pushed to the back of his mind.

"The victim's name may be John Anderson," Manny continued. "Pete Peterson, known to many as Daytona Pete, intercepted a mayday call on his ham radio yesterday afternoon around 5:30 from a man who identified himself as John Anderson. Peterson alerted the New Smyrna Beach Coast Guard Station. That was it. The airwaves went silent. The mayday call came at the height of the storm. The coast guard chopper out of Savannah spotted the boat about three o'clock this morning. A couple of early-morning beach strollers also spotted the stranded boat. They called the NSB police, who in turn called the coast guard."

"That's all?" Fred asked.

"Almost. The exterior of the yacht and the decks were washed clean from the waves of the storm. Pelican Bay Marina is sending a crew down to pick up the boat and put her into one of their storage bays. There's still quite a bit of water in the galley. The name painted on the stern is Molly C. We found no information such as city, state, or country registration. Also, here's a piece of rope that was tied to a rail on the stern," Manny said, handing Dani the brown paper bag. "She's no small ketch at forty-four feet long. There's a nice captain's deck and living room. She could probably sleep six. I also notified Agent Hutchinson."

"Yes," George said, "no telling where the murder took place. From what you said about the mayday call, it probably happened out in the ocean but close to our shore."

"Fred and George, go down to the beach. See what you can learn. Did anyone see the boat come ashore? If you find anything as to its origin, call Dani. Dani, I want you to start a search for the boat's registration. My guess is that the salvage crew will take the better part of today, maybe even tomorrow, to get her to float. I'm going to visit Daytona Pete."

Peaches looked up as Sam entered the bullpen. "Good morning, everyone. My, what a fearsome group. Just thought I would drive back here and stretch my legs a little, so to speak," Sam said with a chuckle.

Sam Houston had been with the DBPD for twenty years, most of that time as the county medical examiner. Now at fifty, he still exuded enthusiasm about his profession. The scientific breakthroughs that seemed to happen every day were exciting. A somewhat portly man, he stood a short five-foot-eight. His hair, prematurely silver, accentuated his pale blue eyes. A faint Aussie accent could be detected at the end of a long day.

"I took this picture of the victim's arm," Sam said. "He has a strange tattoo just below the left shoulder. It could be a religious symbol, a gang code of arms, or just a graphic he liked. My guess it's religious in origin. Not sure what it means."

Sam passed the picture around to the group. Dani was last in line. "What a cool tattoo," she mused. "Kinda like a caricature of a bird, a condor. They're birds of prey, a vulture-type of bird, you know. This *looks* harmless, rather cute with its blue tail feathers fanned out, yellow beak. He appears to be dressed in a little red, white, and blue jacket trimmed in gold. However, there's nothing cute about those gold talons. They could rip you apart."

Chapter 5

— •••—

"WE INTERRUPT THIS PROGRAM with breaking news out of New Smyrna Beach.

Police report that a forty-four-foot yacht named the Molly C was beached last night during the fierce storm that whipped through the area. A man, thought to be in his forties, was found entangled in the boat's cleat with a bullet wound in the head. There was no identification on the body.

The John Doe was transported to the Volusia County morgue. The boat is said to be lolling in the surf, but rescue efforts are underway to free her and take her to Pelican Bay Marina in Daytona Beach.

Channel 13 News will update you on this developing story as we receive additional information. Now back to the weather."

Chapter 6

— • • • —

CATHERINE HAINSWORTH SWITCHED OFF the television set. "I bet Manny's on the case," she said to her housekeeper. "I'm off to an appointment, Lucy. The gardener may be over today to assess the damage from last night's storm. See you later."

"Have a nice day, Miss Catherine. Dinner will be in the refrigerator, ready for you to warm up whenever you get home."

As Catherine backed her BMW out of the garage, she took a quick look to see if any debris littered the driveway. Nothing seemed to be in her path so she turned around and pulled into the street. The spring sunshine gave no hint of the dark ominous clouds of yesterday. Catherine, an architect, had been widowed for three years. She was now back in the workforce at Stone & Associates, a prominent architectural firm. She enjoyed her job, eating up the assignments Russell Stone gave her. In fact, at thirty-five, her designs were winning awards and bringing new clients to the firm. This morning, however, she was making a stop at the bead shop before going on to work.

Tillie Brown, the owner of the House of Beads in Ormond Beach on Granada Avenue, had called Catherine regarding a business opportunity. The shop next to hers was vacant, and she was considering expanding into the space. She wanted Catherine's advice.

With the temperature mild, Catherine opened the windows of her car to let in the fresh, rain-washed breeze as she drove. She always enjoyed a trip to the little bead shop, even though it still brought back memories of the awful day when Russell Stone's wife died there.

"Stop it," she mumbled. She was determined to transfer her thoughts to the day's schedule ahead, but her mind returned to the story about the boat, and the murdered man, and then to Manny. Dear Manny—her friend since high school.

Catherine pulled into the plaza where the bead shop was located. Crews of men were clearing two large trees that had fallen from the median strip surrounding the plaza. They sawed the trunks into manageable lengths and then scooped the pieces into a dump truck. She was glad she had pulled on a pair of dark-wash jeans, topped with a white T-shirt and cropped red jacket. Not sure of what she would run into on the road, she dressed casually for the appointment. Red sandals peeked out from the legs of the jeans. Her blonde hair was pulled back into a ponytail. Suits were her usual attire. She was a consummate professional.

Locking her car, she headed for the shop. The tinkle of the little silver bell alerted Tillie that she had arrived.

"Catherine, right on time as usual," Tillie said, handing a string of clear crystal beads to a customer. "I'll be with you in a minute. Help yourself to coffee. It's a new blend, almond mocha."

"Thanks. I will. It smells wonderful. Don't hurry. You know I love to see what's new." Catherine went into the cozy classroom and poured herself a cup of coffee, adding a thimble-size portion of cream. She then walked back into the main part of the shop and the sparkle of the beads.

"Catherine, it's so good to see you," Tillie said. "Sorry for the delay. Before any more customers come in, let's go next door so I can show you the space. I have a key."

As the two women went out the door, Tillie turned to Catherine. "Did you hear the news this morning? Terrible about that boat, and a man found murdered, for heaven's sake. It must have been an awful sight."

"Yes, I did. I'm sure Manny's on the case," Catherine said.

"Maybe that handsome Washington agent of yours—"

"Tillie, whatever are you saying? He's not my agent."

Tillie smiled. "Well, you certainly knew who I was referring to."

Catherine followed Tillie to the shop next door. She was now all business and making note of what possibilities might be reasonable for expansion. The facade of the space was identical to the bead shop. Both had two picture windows. *An awning across the two shops would tie them together,* she thought. Tillie unlocked the door, and the two women went in.

"Tillie, what did you have in mind? Are you thinking of cutting a doorway to link the two shops?"

"Oh, yes," Tillie said. "I would want a doorway."

"Do you think your business can support doubling your space? Could you run more classes? Do you need more wall area to display the beads?" Catherine asked as she walked around sipping her coffee.

"I have an opportunity to add vintage pieces to my stock. What I mean is, over the years I've been collecting and repairing old jewelry— a stone lost from a bracelet, a clip or pin missing on the back of a wonderful brooch."

Catherine walked to one of the picture windows and looked out at the parking lot. "Tillie, the plaza seems to be doing well. It has a good mix of businesses, anchored with the supermarket, some retail, a restaurant, bagel shop. I didn't notice any other vacant space, which is unusual nowadays. Lots of foot traffic, business people, tourists, and students from nearby colleges. What would you think of using some of the space for a Wi-Fi cyber café?"

"I've used the services of a cyber café on trips," Tillie replied, her head tilted in concentration. "What's Wi-Fi?"

"It's a wireless network," Catherine replied. "Customers can bring their laptops equipped with wireless capability and use your network. Usually a wire connection to the network is also available. Salespeople can stop for a cup of coffee and update their files or lookup potential customers. You could also offer a few workstations and charge an hourly rate. Some of those cyber customers may take a look at your beads, men buying a kit or a class for a woman in their lives, or something they're designing for themselves."

"Well now. You have my mind spinning with new ideas. But I don't have enough money, I'm sure, to launch such an ambitious venture."

"Tell you what. You play with the idea. Let your thoughts run wild. I'll do the same thing. Keep your juices flowing and visit a couple of cyber cafes in nearby towns. Contact the owner of the building and find out the rent or if it's for sale. Ask them for the right of first refusal. If they want some money in escrow to hold it for a couple of weeks, let me know. I've been looking for an investment opportunity, and, Tillie, you may have found one for me."

Chapter 7

—•••—

DAYTONA PETE'S CONDO building stood seven stories high on the edge of the Atlantic Ocean. Manny parked his black SUV and, with Peaches at his side, entered the building. They were greeted by a short doorman wearing a dark green uniform. "I'm here to see William Peterson. I understand he's on the seventh floor. Do you know if he's in?" Manny asked.

"I don't know any William Peterson," the man said.

"Daytona Pete?"

"Oh yes, sir. Daytona Pete is up there. Just take that elevator. When the door slides back, you'll be facing his front door."

Manny and Peaches rode up on the elevator and stepped out onto the seventh floor. True to the man's word, Unit 702, in gold letters on the door, faced them. Taking note of the freshly-painted cream-colored walls and thick dark brown Berber carpet, Manny rang the bell.

"Hang on, I'll be right there," a man behind the door yelled.

The owner of the voice opened the door. He was sitting in a wheelchair—a double amputee, both legs missing just below the knee. "Yep, what can I do for you?"

"My name is Captain Manny Salinas, Daytona Beach Police Department. Are you Daytona Pete?" Manny asked, with a wide grin. "I understand you intercepted a mayday call yesterday."

"Well, hell, come on in. Chuck said someone from the department would be stopping by. And who is this?" Pete asked scratching Peaches behind the ears. The dog loved Pete's attention. She planted herself as close as she could get to the wheelchair, putting her paw up on his right stump.

"This is Peaches. She must like you because she's doesn't voluntarily shake hands with someone unless they ask."

"Come on in, Captain Salinas. I just put on a pot of coffee." Daytona Pete did a wheelie and headed for the open kitchen area.

"Please, call me Manny."

"Manny it is. And, knock off the Daytona—just call me Pete. Do you put anything in this syrup? Sorry, I always make it strong. Something I got used to in Iraq."

"Cream and sugar if you have it."

Daytona Pete, a veteran, lost his legs below the knee from a land mine. Prosthetics were fitted for legs but he never bothered to attach them when he was at home. With his savings, disability, and mustering out pay, he bought a condo overlooking the Atlantic Ocean in Daytona Beach Shores. It was a very small community bordering Port Orange. The only claim to a downtown area was a 7-Eleven convenience store and a few tourist shops.

The condo's balcony, wheelchair accessible, faced the ocean and captured whatever breeze was coming through that hour, that day. The pelicans rode the breeze in the morning and then again late afternoon, diving into the water for their breakfast and dinner.

Pete's condo, being on the seventh floor, afforded him particularly good reception on his ham radio and cell phone. A relay tower was within a mile and was aligned perfectly with the satellites racing around the earth.

"This is quite a place you have. I thought my equipment was sophisticated, but you have me beat. What's with the three computer monitors?" Manny asked.

"Well, my hobby is communicating with passing ships. Normally I can't see them as they're over the horizon, but I can talk to them and they to me. My passion, however, is betting on the horses over the Internet. With three monitors, I can watch and bet on three different tracks simultaneously, watching each race in real time, say Aqueduct in New York. Gulfstream Park, Florida. Hell, even Australia and Dubai come through loud and clear."

Pete handed Manny a cup of coffee and took a sip of his own.

"My living room is set up like a command center for my racing hobby. I call it my OTBP, off-track betting parlor," Pete said chuckling. "I have an account on a wagering website for the horses. I deposit funds into this account, an online transfer from my bank here in Florida. The website gives me access to tracks around the world, and it's all legal, Captain. You should try it sometime."

"The only time I bet on the horses was at Calder in Miami. I lost my shirt, but I have to admit I had fun doing it."

"Please excuse the mess of papers, Manny. I'm getting ready for the first leg of the Triple Crown in two weeks, the Kentucky Derby. I've been collecting all the stats for the horses, again pulling information from my wagering site, but I also check in with various racing gurus. Then I'll handicap the field. How's your coffee? Want more cream?"

"No. This is great. I probably won't sleep for a month."

Peaches settled down behind the sliding glass doors to the balcony. Her head was between her paws, but her eyes darted back and forth watching the pelicans fly by.

"I had some good luck while in the army, as well as some not so good luck," Pete remarked, patting his leg. "While taking the standard psych tests, a shrink noticed that I had the ability to see obscure patterns within written text, and within a series of seemingly random numbers. Where others saw randomness, I saw patterns. As a kid, I was always making up my own codes. Well, the shrink recommended me for crypto school. After graduation, the army assigned me to a cryptology sub-specialty designation. Hell, I should have stayed a cryptologist." Pete patted his thigh again.

"I guess that skill would come in handy when looking at all the statistics you compile," Manny said, gazing around at all the pieces of paper. "However, much as I would like to hear more about the horses, I think I'd better ask you a few questions about the call you intercepted yesterday. Looking out your balcony now, it's hard to believe how bad the storm was."

"The call came in late in the afternoon, around 5:30," Pete said. "I wasn't doing anything with the computer, just looking out at the angry sea, black clouds, and rain blowing sideways. Fact is I dozed off. The crackle of my ham radio woke me up. Then I heard, 'mayday, mayday,' loud and clear. I looked out the doors but couldn't see any boat. So I hustled over to the radio, grabbed the mike, and asked who was calling and their location. The guy said his name was John Anderson and the boat was the Molly C. He said they ran out of fuel and were taking on water. He thought he was near Ponce Inlet lighthouse, but he couldn't see because of the storm."

"This man, John Anderson, he used the word 'we' and 'they'?" Manny asked.

"Yes, he did. I know when Chuck, my friend at the Coast Guard Station, called me later, he said they found a man on board, shot dead and no sign of another person. Shit, I'm getting ahead of myself. Anyway I called the coast guard immediately. They're used to getting calls from me. Mostly just chatting, but sometimes it's serious. Chuck stops by once in a while and we go out for a beer. Anyway, he said they, too, had heard the call."

"What channel did this John Anderson's call come in on?'

"The distress channel, sixteen."

"Did you hear from Anderson again?"

"Nope. Just dead air. Couldn't raise him, and neither could Chuck."

"Well, he and the boat did exist. It was definitely the Molly C, but the man had no ID on him. We can't verify that John Doe is John Anderson or someone else. The boat's being traced to see if we can find some answers. Who owns it? Where she's registered? If you think of anything else, please give me a call. Here's my card with my cell number."

Manny took his empty coffee cup to the kitchen counter. Sensing her master was about to leave, Peaches was instantly on her feet. "When you think about the call, try to remember any background sounds you heard. It doesn't matter how insignificant you think it might be. Right now, you are our only link to that voice."

"Sorry, Manny. The static was fierce. I was lucky to pick up the communication at all."

Chapter 8

— • • • —

THE SCENE AT THE BEACH looked like something out of Gulliver's Travels. Sunbathers, gawkers, and interested bystanders filled the area around the yacht. The police kept shouting at them to keep back. Flagler Avenue's beach access road was now a ribbon of sand twenty-feet wide leading to the boat. The police monitored the strip to keep the path open. A coast guard helicopter, as well as several choppers from the news channels, circled overhead.

Three huge cranes, a couple of bulldozers, and a heavy-duty tractor circled the stranded yacht. The water held a flotilla of various sized boats, including a couple of rubber rafts. All spectators waited to see how the salvage crew was going to rescue the boat from the sandbar.

The noisy, chaotic scene greeted Fred and George as they drove through the strip with their squad car's yellow light whirling.

"Would you look at that?" Fred said. "You'd think this was the first time they've seen a boat washed up on the shore around here."

George parked the white squad car next to a van from Pelican Bay Marina. The Atlantic's waves were gently lapping the shore. "Can you tell me who's in charge here?" George yelled to an NSB uniformed officer.

"Over there. The guy in dark blue overalls," the officer yelled back over the noise of the choppers and the engines of the equipment.

Fred and George made their way to the dark overalls and introduced themselves. All conversation was held at a high decibel level.

"Ted Adams, Pelican Bay Marina," Ted said, extending his hand to Fred and George. "Glad you boys came down."

"How does it look to get her out in one piece?" George asked, still talking in a loud voice.

"Hopefully, we can. We're getting her ready. You can see the lines from each side being pulled out to the barge, and from there to that tug. We'll be ready when the tide starts to turn back. She has water in the galley, but we think it's from the storm and not from a hole in the hull."

"We have some forensic work to do on her," George said. "Can you check if the water is from a leak? We can't take a chance she'll sink."

"Sure," Ted replied. "My men were about to do just that. They're bringing the pump over now. If she stays dry we can proceed with Plan A—tow her to our marina and put her up on one of the storage bays for you. If she draws water, we go to plan B."

"What will that be?" Fred asked.

"Let her sit where she is until you guys say you're done. At which point we may have to break her up for scrap," Ted replied.

Fred and George climbed the rope ladder and started going over every inch of the Molly C they could. Ted's men hauled up a pump connected to a generator on the beach below. It didn't take long to pump out the last of the water from the lower area. No hole was visible from the inside or the outside. They wouldn't know for sure whether the hull was ruptured until she was in the water. With tools from his forensic kit, George took three samples of blood spattered in the galley area. Then all they could do was wait.

Fred and George figured they had an hour before the operation to pull her free from her entrapment would begin. They decided to mingle with the bystanders to see if they could find anyone who was on the beach the night before or anyone who saw the Molly C slam onto the shore. Their efforts were fruitless. They found no one, at least no one who would come forward.

The two detectives decided to grab a burger at the Breakers, a restaurant bordering the access road and the beach. It was a very popular place serving fish, blackened, grilled, poached, and baked, but burgers were their specialty. Windows lined the restaurant's 100-foot frontage. A long narrow counter was fastened to the wall underneath the windows. High stools marched along under the counter affording patrons a panoramic view of the beach and ocean beyond. The counter was definitely the best seat in the house to observe bikini-clad girls.

Fred and George each ordered a burger and a large ice tea. The two plain-clothes detectives chatted quietly about the operation going on down the beach and occasionally remarked about a girl's bathing suit, or lack thereof.

They were interrupted by a teenage boy busing the counter. "I saw the whole thing last night," the boy said, gazing out the window.

Turning to see who was talking, George asked, "What time was that, son?"

"I stay real late to mop the floors after we close down at night. So it was about 2:30 in the morning. I was mopping, and sometimes, when there was a big bolt of lightning, I'd look out. Well, there were several bolts at the same time. They really lit up the sky. Then I saw her. She was just a few yards from the beach. I thought she'd stay out, but it wasn't long until she washed up on the shore riding a gigantic wave."

"Then what happened? Did you see anybody on her?" Fred asked.

"No, I didn't see anybody, but after a while a chopper flew over her several times. It was a coast guard helicopter."

"What did you do?" Fred asked.

"Nothin. Because of the chopper, I didn't report it. I went home when I finished the floors. I just now came back to work."

"We might want to talk to you again, young man. You've been very helpful. How can we get in touch with you?" George asked, handing him his card.

"Whoa. You're detectives, huh?" the young man uttered taking the card. He wrote his name and telephone number on the back.

"Thanks," George said. "Here's another one of my cards for you to keep. If you think of anything else give me a call." Fred and George left the restaurant, returning to the enormous task about to commence.

The operation was delicate, but the equipment was huge, powerful. Large engines revved up ready to push the Molly C back into the water. Ted assigned two men aboard to watch if water came into the chamber below or to signal other weak spots, in which case, the mission would be aborted immediately.

The stage was set and the play commenced. The various engines groaned as they pushed and pulled. The Molly C didn't budge. Ted gave the signal a second time. The shoulders of the forklifts pushed, the tugs in the water pulled, the cranes lifted. Slowly the Molly C started to move. All of the equipment kept up the pressure. Then gentle as you please, she slid off the sandbar and began floating on the water. The tugs kept pulling. The bystanders stood gaping, then let out a cheer. The Molly C was saved from the scrap heap.

Ted's men gave the all clear sign—no water seeping in from below. One tug dropped out of the procession. The other tug came alongside the yacht to hold her fast and headed north to Pelican Bay Marina. Fred and George shook hands with Ted. "Good job, man," George said. "The NSB officer will stay on the boat to protect the crime scene. One of our men will relieve him as soon as you put her up in the storage bay. We'll see you up at the marina tomorrow morning. Let's hope we can find some clues as to the skipper's identity and where she came from."

As the Molly C receded from view, the beach people went back to sunbathing, frolicking in the gentle surf, and generally enjoying the tranquil sunny day.

Chapter 9

— ● ● ● —

"WELCOME TO CHANNEL 13 mid-day report with breaking news.

Updating our story from this morning, the beached yacht, the Molly C, is still stranded on the shore of New Smyrna. Crews from a local marina and the coast guard are working to free her from her resting point. As you can see from our Channel 13 chopper, two tugs are pulling with all their might. She seems to be inching ever so slowly off the sandbar into the water. Over two-hundred spectators are reportedly watching the operation.

And there she goes. The tugs are pulling her out to sea away from the shallow water of the shore. She's floating freely. The crowd is cheering. Many waving their hands, towels, or shirts as the Molly C begins her trek north.

Authorities tell us she will be moved to Ponce Inlet and then up the Halifax River to Pelican Bay Marina.

No word yet as to the identification of the body found entangled on the boat. He appeared to have died from a gunshot wound. We will update you as this story develops. But for now, the Molly C is afloat."

— ● ● ● —

"DAMN. THE JOB WAS BUNGLED and now the operation is compromised. That bastard cost us thousands of dollars, money we desperately needed. One good thing, the skipper can't talk," the man said from the shadows of the room.

"What do we do if they find the stuff?" another man said, pacing nervously around the room.

"We make sure they don't. Get to the marina tomorrow. Check out the situation. Then we'll talk."

Chapter 10

—•••—

FOR SOME, FRIDAY was the end of a work week. However, Manny and his team knew they would not be having a weekend barbeque which was a shame because the day was perfect—white puffy clouds helped to keep the temperature in the mid-seventies with low humidity. Manny, with Peaches sitting in the front seat next to him, drove straight to the marina to check the condition of the Molly C.

Fred and George followed behind. Ted Adams was waiting for the men and immediately took them to the boat to undergo a thorough forensic inspection.

"I put her in the far bay, first level," Ted said. "That berth will give you easy access and privacy. She made it here just fine and doesn't appear to have sustained any damage. I didn't go aboard."

"Thanks, Ted. Your crew did a helluva job yesterday," Manny said. He and Peaches walked down a tree-lined path to the storage facility. Large cranes with davits, chains, and other pulleys were at the far end of the building.

"I'm anxious to take a look at this baby," Fred said, as he and George followed Manny.

"Me, too," George replied. "Let's see how the other half lives."

The men climbed the wooden stairs to a walkway. Planks ran along the side of the yacht's brass rail facilitating their boarding. With an easy leap, Peaches joined her master on the deck. Boarding a boat was now part of her DNA since living with Manny on his houseboat. The three men put on white latex gloves and began their careful inspection of the Molly C. George swept the stern and opened all the built-in compartments. Fred took the lower level, sleeping quarters, and the galley. Manny and Peaches went to the cockpit.

Manny had a theory he wanted to investigate with Peaches. Ever since Peaches alerted him to a body in the trunk of a car, he suspected that his adopted stray had received special training. Manny knew that working dogs were trained to respond to voice commands rather than hand signs. A handler didn't want his dog to look away from the bad guy to get a signal. Manny was convinced over the last few months that Peaches indeed had K9 military training. He let Peaches roam the area to do her thing.

Manny opened a cabinet door. The shelves contained several folded maps with a box of tissue on top. He called Peaches over and ran his hand around the inside of the cabinet. Peaches stuck her nose inside the opening. She sniffed a couple of times, then backed away and sat down looking at her master. Her tail thumped on the carpeted floor. "Looks like you think this is a game, girl," Manny said, giving the dog's silky head several pets. "Well, okay, my friend, let's go play."

Manny repeated the game with all the cabinets in the cockpit. He and Peaches then went to the lower deck. He passed George, who came in to help Fred.

Systematically checking every nook and cranny with Peaches, Manny entered the last area, the forward stateroom. He walked Peaches around the perimeter of the room. He opened closet doors and built-in cabinets. Nothing. "Well, I guess that's it, girl. Maybe you don't have a trained nose after all, or maybe there's nothing to smell," Manny said, sitting down on the bed.

Peaches jumped on the bed beside him. Suddenly she scratched at the bedspread, then jumped down and began pawing at the platform holding the mattress. Down on her front paws, hind end in the air, she scampered around the edges of the bed, whining.

"Hey, Fred, George, come in here, the forward stateroom," Manny yelled.

The two detectives hustled through the narrow hallway and entered the room.

"Help me with this mattress, will you?" Manny requested.

Peaches continued her frenetic actions around the edge of the bed. The men lifted the mattress, setting it against the wall. The platform had drawers accessible from each side. But in the center, on top of the platform were three-hinged compartment doors with recessed handles. The doors appeared to be approximately three feet wide by one foot. Each door was attached to the surface with a piano hinge. Peaches jumped on the platform pawing at the three doors, first one then the other, whining again.

Manny ordered Peaches down off the raised surface. She jumped down and sat, looking expectantly up at her master, back to the platform continuing to voice her interest in the bed.

"Fred, let's see what we have here," Manny said, lifting the door handle closest to the head of the bed.

"Will you look at that?" George said. "Someone must really be pissed losing this cargo. It wouldn't surprise me if we have some visitors soon, real soon."

The space contained many packages of a white substance, each in the shape of a brick. Each brick was wrapped in clear plastic, and all were neatly stacked in the compartment.

Peaches barked softly, never moving from her sitting position, ears up, body tense.

"Fred, you and George go ahead and open the other two doors." Manny stepped back, giving Peaches a scratch behind the ears. Peaches looked up at her master, tongue hanging out, leaning into his thigh.

"This cabinet's loaded, the same as the first," George reported, moving on to the third door.

"Whoa," Fred said. "We have something different here, a metal box along with the bricks."

"Don't touch anything," Manny said, sharply. "We don't know what we're dealing with."

The three men stared down at what each in their own minds estimated was a drug bust of thousands of dollars. With over thirty years of experience between them, the detectives were sure the brick packages did not contain flour or sugar to bake up a batch of cookies.

"I'll call Dani," Manny said, "and ask her to bring the proper equipment to pick up one of the bricks and this metal box. After we know what this stuff is we'll decide how to proceed. It's for sure DEA will get involved. While I call Dani, you two close the doors and put the bedding back in place."

Fred and George closed the cabinets, wrestled the mattress back on top of the frame, and replaced the bedding. Manny walked out to the aft deck and called Dani. While talking to her, he noted the officer he assigned to guard the crime scene standing at the bottom of the stairs. After his call to Dani, he rejoined Fred and George in the stateroom.

"Dani's on her way. Now, as I see it we may, I say *may,* have an opportunity as well as a dilemma. I doubt our John Doe worked alone. With the television news coverage, it's also probable that whoever he worked with knows what happened to this boat, as well as knows where it is, and that a man was found shot to death on it. In fact, as you said, George, I bet we're being watched. If we're careful, our actions can appear to be routine. This yacht is a crime scene. A team would automatically board to get whatever forensic material it could, and then the vessel would be released."

"If we're *real* careful," Fred added, "whoever is watching might think we didn't find the stash and could wait until the boat was released."

"Okay," George said, "but in the meantime, someone may claim the boat. After all, we don't know if the skipper, John Anderson, AKA John Doe, owned the boat, or if he was only bringing the stash to rendezvous with someone else."

"One thing we do know for sure," Manny said, "we keep everything to ourselves. We only talk to people on a need-to-know basis. At this moment, that includes the three of us and Dani. After she verifies what the substance is and what's in the box, then we add to our circle as warranted. Agent Hutchinson hasn't said if he is interested in the case, but I bet he will be after we verify the substance."

"The big issue in front of us," Fred said, "is to secure the crime scene without calling undue attention, so that no one can check to see if the stuff is still on board."

"Right," Manny said. "I told Dani to come alone and to bring a small hazmat bag but big enough for one of the bricks and that other small metal box. I say brick because it appears to be cocaine except for that box. I'm going to talk to the officer on duty and explain that the boat will be taped as a crime scene and that under no circumstances is anyone to board her."

"George and I can do the taping when we leave," Fred said.

"I'll go back to the department," Manny said. "I don't want any slip up on the around-the-clock security. You two stay to help Dani. When she's finished I want everyone back to the department. As soon as she identifies the substance, we'll meet in the bullpen. She'll have to come back after our meeting to dust for fingerprints, as well as to gather a few more blood samples from the galley to add to what you collected yesterday. George, toss me that little yellow-satin pillow on the dresser. If anybody is watching me leave with Peaches, I don't want him to think she found anything."

Manny and Peaches left the stateroom for the aft deck. Once they were outside, he tossed the little pillow to Peaches. She jumped catching it in mid-air and immediately brought it to Manny. "Good, girl," he said, praising the dog in a loud voice. They stepped off the boat onto the plank walkway, and down the stairs to the ground. Once again Manny threw the pillow in the air. Peaches caught the plaything and raced back to Manny. Her body quivered with excitement over the game.

"Your dog sure loves to play," the officer said, smiling as Manny threw the little pillow again.

Chapter 11

—•••—

DANI JUDGED THE DISTANCE from the plank walkway to the deck of the Molly C. Graceful was not a description a bystander would have used to describe her leap. The uniformed officer, now stationed on the aft deck, turned his head away so Dani could not see his smiley face.

"Hello, sir," Dani said, flashing her badge as she gained her footing. The officer knew who she was, but protocol always wins out. "If you'll excuse me, I need some samples for the lab. Are Detectives Watson and Anderson aboard?"

"Yes, ma'am. They're both inside."

"Fred. George," Dani called, heading down the narrow stairway into the galley.

"Keep coming," George called back, leaving the stateroom to meet her.

"Hi, guys. Watcha got? Manny sounded a little mysterious."

"Wait till you see this," Fred said, as he and George dismantled the bed. George opened the third door, and Dani stepped forward to get a better look inside. She nearly stumbled In surprise at the quantity of the stash.

"When's this scheduled to be transported to the department?" she asked, calculations streaming through her head.

"We don't know yet," Fred replied. "Manny wants to see what you come up with. As soon as you know for sure what's wrapped in these packages, we're to huddle back in the bullpen."

"The same kind of bricks you see here are also behind the other two doors," George said, "with the exception of that box."

"Okay. You guys clear out and close the door just in case one of these packs breaks. I brought my special shirt, gloves, and mask," Dani said, pulling the zipper on her case. "I'm not going to check the stuff here. I'll put one brick and this box into my hazmat bag and crack it open back in my lab."

Dani carefully picked up one of the bricks, put it in a sealed container and placed it into her bag. She repeated the procedure with the small metal box. With this part of her task completed, she removed another brick that was underneath the one she put in her bag. Seeing that there was still another layer, she carefully removed one more brick.

The bottom of the hold now visible, she returned the two bricks to the compartment and then added up the number of packages stored in the cabinet, thirty-six in all. Assuming that the other compartments held the same number, the total number of bricks was potentially 108. Dani slowly removed her special clothing and backed away from what she calculated as a street value of nearly three-million dollars.

"Okay, guys. You can come back in," she called, giving an all-clear rap on the stateroom door.

With Dani's help, Fred and George reassembled the bed—the mattress on top, as well as sheets, two blankets, a bedspread, and two pillows. When they shut the door behind them, the room was neat and tidy, ready for guests and a good night's sleep.

"See you fellows later," Dani said absentmindedly. She still couldn't believe the quantity of bricks she'd seen.

Fred and George sealed the entrance to the interior of the yacht with yellow crime-scene tape and then left the marina.

Dani drove back to the department and went straight to her lab. A short time later, and after performing a few tests on the contents of the plastic-wrapped brick and the metal container, she leaned back in her chair and softly exclaimed, "Holy shit."

Manny heard the utterance as he entered the lab. "It must be good," Manny said.

Dani looked over to him. Her face turned white as the blood drained away. She stared back at Manny with wide eyes and said, "The metal box contains the deadly toxin ricin."

Chapter 12

— • • • —

FRED AND GEORGE STRAGGLED into the bullpen taking note of Peaches asleep on her pillow beside Manny's desk. Manny stood at the case board making notes. It was Saturday, 7:30 a.m.

"Morning, Captain," Fred said, sipping from a fresh, tall, insulated cup of steaming coffee.

George knelt down to give Peaches a nice rub behind her ears. She returned the favor with a sloppy kiss on his cheek.

"Where's Dani? Didn't she get the message about our think tank session?" Manny asked.

"Yes, she got the message," Dani said, "and she's here in body, but until she downs her large cup of this nerve zapper, the mind may be a casual observer." She flopped into her chair, swiveling around to face the group.

"Late night, Princess?" George asked.

"Knock it off, Anderson. I had a late night date with a petri dish," she replied, taking a long drag on her coffee mug.

"Hey, where is everybody?" The big male voice preceded his body.

"Hutch," Manny said. "So you decided to come down. You must have had a heck of a tail wind."

"Welcome back, Hutch," Fred and George chimed in shaking the agent's hand.

"Your timing is perfect, Hutch. We checked out the yacht and wait until we fill you in on what we found," Dani said.

Manny hit the save button on the electronic whiteboard. "Okay, boys and girls, here's what we've got. One John Doe shot in the head. One yacht, Molly C, origin unknown, in dry-dock at Pelican Bay Marina. 216 pounds of cocaine with a street value of nearly three-million dollars, and a cup of ricin—enough to contaminate thousands of people."

"Ricin?" Hutch said. "Holy shit."

"I believe Dani uttered those same two words a few hours ago," Manny said.

"Whoa," Hutch exclaimed. "With what you've told me so far, and especially with the presence of ricin, that storm may have blown in some kind of terrorist plot."

—•••—

Manny went to his desk and unscrewed the cap of his half-full bottle of cold water. After a long swallow, he said, "Daytona Pete, he wants to be called Pete, is a wildcard at this point."

"Wildcard my foot," Hutch said. "He's one helluva man. He and I met up on a mission in Iraq, just before he lost his legs. I heard he intercepted the mayday call."

Hutch popped the lid of his second large cup of coffee. "What's your guess, Manny? Would you say John Doe either knew what he was carrying and was eliminated, or he didn't know what he was carrying? In which case, whoever put the stuff on the boat felt the need to get rid of him. Either way, whoever put the drugs on the Molly C must be frantic and will try to recover the stuff."

Manny went back to his desk for another marker. He had written so furiously that the first pen's ink ran out. "The story of the beached boat and her recovery has been all over the news here in Florida. The AP picked it up as a compelling story when the salvage crew tried to free the boat from the sandbar. The story then flashed over the U.S. as well as other countries. This includes the fact that an unidentified victim of a gunshot wound was found on board. Yes, Hutch, I'd say it is a good bet that whoever put the stuff on the boat wants to recover it. The same people may or may not be responsible for John Doe's murder. With this in mind, I've thought of a plan to draw out the smugglers."

"Good," Hutch said. "Let's hear it."

Manny again walked to his desk, but this time to take a swig of the now warm water from his bottle. "I think we can use the notoriety of the story to our advantage. We keep the news of the cocaine and the ricin out of the news. We guard that secret like it's pure gold. The perps won't know if we found the stuff or not. In fact, they may feel lucky and assume we haven't discovered the drugs. So how do we get them to tip their hand?" Manny asked. "More publicity," he said, answering his own question.

"The Chamber of Commerce Charity Auction is scheduled in two weeks here in Daytona Beach. It's a perfect time to honor two of our citizens. One, Daytona Pete for his interception of the mayday call, as well as his aiding several other ships over the course of the years. Two, Peaches is already being honored at the event for her assistance in the capture of Julie Stone's killer, Russell Stone's wife, last month. Daytona Pete will be our bait. Being he's an Iraq war vet, and even though he's in a wheelchair, I wouldn't want to mess with him. He can easily handle this assignment. We'll try to lure the terrorists into contacting Pete about accessing the Molly C."

"I like it," George said sitting forward, enthusiastically cracking his knuckles.

"Well, it could work," Hutch said. "It can't hurt to try, because right now we don't have anything else to go on. However, I think we need an all out effort to find where that boat came from. We also have to get the bricks off the Molly C just in case the perps try something. We don't want to take any chances on them getting control of the stuff."

"I figured there are a total of 108 bricks," Dani said. "At two pounds each, we have 216 pounds of coke to remove. How about we plan a photo opportunity *without* the media? We'll take Pete to the boat. Make a fuss over him and at the same time switch the bricks with flour. I can shoot a video of Pete, which I'll feed to the media after the fact. Heck, all they care about are the pictures anyway. We can do the exchange anytime you give the nod."

"The sooner the better," Hutch said, mulling over Dani's plan.

The wastebasket sounded a light thud, as it received one large empty coffee cup. "I'll work out the details," Dani said, extremely pleased that Hutch saw merit in her idea.

Chapter 13

—•••—

Twelve days to the Kentucky Derby

DAYTONA PETE WAS CURSING up a storm. He couldn't find the report he downloaded the night before. The Kentucky Derby was quickly approaching and he had to have the preliminary information on the horses in order to start his ritual. The ritual of building his winning wagers included wearing his yellow T-shirt imprinted with the head of a racehorse. The ring of the doorbell added to his irritation.

"Who is it?" he shouted.

"Quit your cussing you SOB, and open this door."

Pete looked up. "No. It can't be," he said to himself. He performed a perfect pirouette in his wheelchair and opened the door. "Son of a B," Pete said. "It is you, you old codger."

Hutch leaned over and gave his old friend a bear hug. "Watch how you address me," Hutch said, fishing out a cold bottle of Corona beer from one of the pockets of his cargo pants. "And, that's not all I have for you. How about this little green treasure? A lime to go with that favorite beer of yours."

"You make me want to cry with happiness," Pete said, taking the beer and the lime to the kitchen sink. He immediately cut the lime into wedges, opened the bottle, stuffed a wedge inside, and took a long drink. "Ah, now that's a brew."

Manny and Peaches slid in behind Hutch and closed the door. Peaches would not let Hutch have all the fun. She muscled her way between the two and put her paw up on Pete's stump. "Yes, I see you," Pete said, scratching his furry visitor behind the ears. Satisfied, she went to the balcony door and took up her post watching the pelicans diving into the Atlantic Ocean.

"So are you guys going to tell me what this social call is about?" Pete asked. "Something *real* social I surmise, as I'm being bribed with my favorite beer."

"Good old Pete. No chit-chat. Get to the grit of the matter," Hutch said grinning. "Okay, you asked for it. Have you maintained your top secret clearance?"

"Uh oh. Now I know I'm in for trouble. And, the answer is yes, I still carry my top secret clearance from the Army."

"I figured you did. Manny and I are reading you into an operation. We need your help."

When Hutch said he was "reading him in" Pete knew the operation was big. Stephen Hutchinson definitely had his attention. Fishing two more beers out of his pockets, Hutch gave one to Manny and opened one for himself. Then he and Manny sat down on the couch facing Pete. "Cheers," the three said in unison, raising their bottles to one another.

"It has to do with the mayday call you intercepted a few days ago," Manny said. "As you know there was a dead guy on board, shot in the head. Kinda on board. He was tangled up with the lines on the cleat on the starboard side of the stern. There was no ID on him. The only clue we have as to his identity is the name the guy gave you on your radio, John Anderson."

Manny stopped talking long enough for a sip of his beer. "The boat is at the Pelican Bay Marina. A couple of my detectives and I searched her for clues and possible forensic material. We all came up empty until Peaches over there found a gold mine." At the sound of her name, Peaches looked back over her shoulder, gave a wag of her tail, and then resumed her post. "There were 216 pounds of cocaine and a cup of ricin hidden away inside the platform of the stateroom's bed."

"Holy shit, ricin?" Pete asked.

"That seems to be the favorite expression in this case," Manny said.

"Given the pure powder form they found," Hutch said, "the ricin could be used in several different delivery methods. We think mainly as a mist in the air, like the subway episode in Tokyo. It's possible it was being smuggled here as a weapon component for a very dirty bomb."

Two soft whistles came out of Pete's mouth. "That's bad, bad stuff."

"We have a plan to draw the terrorists out, but we need your help," Hutch said.

"Hey, anything I can do, but I won't be much use to a SWAT team." Pete offered.

"We haven't let the contents of the ship get out. No news story," Manny said. "It's a tightly-guarded secret. We're pretty sure someone is very anxious to get their hands on that cargo."

"Given the size of the shipment and the complexity to deliver such a stash," Hutch broke in, "there's probably a group involved. From the media reports, the terrorists are aware the skipper sent out a mayday call. They know the boat was beached because of the storm, and that there was a dead man. They also know the boat is now located at the marina."

"I noticed the news didn't give out a name," Pete said.

"That's right. We didn't give out the name of the dead guy because as far as we're concerned, he's a John Doe." Manny took another swig of his beer and continued. "The name of the boat was painted on her stern, so they know it's their boat. Our plan is to use you as bait, if you agree, as someone who could have access to the boat, if he so chose."

"What good would that do them or you?" Pete asked.

"First, if they contact you, it gives us a lead as to who they are," Manny said. "Second, you could arrange a meeting, if they indicated it was urgent they get on board. Tell them there is an officer on the boat, but you think you could relieve him on the ground. You work for the police occasionally being a former officer in the Army or something like that. Of course, you want to be paid for your efforts. A cut of the take would be appropriate, don't you think?"

"How would they find out I might be able to help them?" Pete asked, adding another slice of lime to his drink.

"There's a charity auction, a big event in the area, a week from Friday," Manny said. "There will be lots of publicity and even more PR if we honor you and your good works with boats in trouble off the coast. Off *your* coast. We're already giving Peaches an honorary award for her action in taking the killer out in a case we just wrapped up. You might be given second billing so it wouldn't look so obvious."

"Gee, thanks a lot. Second in line after a dog. It's a good thing I like you, Peaches," Pete said, looking over at his new friend.

Hearing Pete talk to her, Peaches came over and put her head in his lap, gently nudging him to give her a pat on the head.

"We'll give out enough information about you in the press release," Manny said, "so without too much trouble they could find you. The story will include that, because you intercepted the mayday call, you feel a kinship of sorts with the Molly C and have visited the marina several times to see if anyone has come forth to claim her. Once this plan starts to go down, I'll leave Peaches here to give you backup."

"Let's see, a week from Friday. I don't have to do anything but be at the auction and here in my condo?" Pete asked.

"That's it," Hutch said. "Manny will pick you up for your appearance at the auction. I'll be there, but in the background."

"Well, then count me in. I'll still be able to prepare for the Derby. Good thing the auction isn't the same day as the Derby, because then I'd have a real problem."

Hutch, knowing his old friend's passion for the horses, said, "I wouldn't dream of disturbing your big plans for a potential triple-crown winner. The auction is an evening affair the day before the Derby. So don't think you're going to weasel out of your chance for fame and fortune, especially since you're sharing the glory with a dog."

"Okay. It's a deal. There's a big horse that's getting a lot of attention, but he hasn't been in many races. Santiago, he's a handicapper whose blog I follow religiously, thinks the horse isn't tested. His name is *Big Brown,* and I'm betting on him to win the Derby."

Chapter 14

—•••—

THE FIRST PERSON on Manny's call list was Catherine Hainsworth, the chairwoman of the charity auction. Manny and Hutch thought it a good idea to honor Pete, but it wouldn't happen unless Catherine approved.

Catherine and Manny went to grade school together, and truth be told, he had carried a crush on her ever since. Catherine had been married to a very wealthy realtor. The marriage produced no children, so when her husband died, Catherine was the sole beneficiary of his estate making her an heiress. She was also a beautiful woman and highly regarded in interior design and architectural development.

"Hi, Cat," Manny said, using his pet name for her since their school days. "I hope I didn't interrupt your work."

"Manny, what a nice surprise, and, no, you didn't interrupt anything. I was outside the kitchen door gathering some herbs from my garden. You caught me playing hooky. How about you? Are you catching more bad guys?"

"Always on the trail, Cat. Always on the trail. I have a proposal I'd like to run by you. Any chance you could meet me at the Aquarium for lunch?" Manny held his breath, hoping she would say yes to his offer. He hadn't seen her in a few weeks. He wished some day he would get up the nerve to ask her for a real date.

"Oh, I love proposals. How could I refuse such an offer?"

"Wonderful. Say about 1:30? We should be able to sit outside on the patio after the lunch crowd leaves."

"That's not much time, but I think I can manage. I'll see you there." Catherine cradled the phone in her hands a second before hanging up, a smile forming on her lips. Suddenly, looking at her watch, she said to herself, "I barely have time to get ready. An hour-and-a-half will simply fly by."

—•••—

MANNY'S TIMING WAS PERFECT. There were several empty tables outside on the deck looking over the water. The Halifax River, an intracoastal waterway, separated the Daytona Beach mainland from the beach side of the city. Today the deep-blue water sparkled in the sunshine as a few sailboats drifted along in the soft breeze. Birds chattered in the old oak tree on the north side of the restaurant, thick Spanish moss hanging from the trees' branches.

The patio of the restaurant faced east so the afternoon sun was far enough on its arc across the sky to afford shade for those sitting outdoors. Manny asked the waiter for a table next to the water's edge but off to the side. He wanted a private conversation with Catherine. *Why do I always get the stomach flutters when I'm going to see her,* he thought? "Come on, Emanuel, you're not a school kid," he muttered under his breath.

"Manny, how wonderful you look," Catherine said as she approached him. He was wearing his signature black trousers secured with belt, holster, and gun, but today he topped it with a tan shirt and black tie in place of his usual black on black. His inky black hair and mustache were matched by his dark, almost black eyes.

He stood up and in his usual fashion with Catherine, and only Catherine, took her hand and softly kissed the top of her delicate knuckles. "Hey, that's my line, but in your case it's true," he said, his lips parting in a smile.

Catherine looked smart in a cream-colored sheath against her Florida tan, her blonde hair pulled back in a twist. She settled herself in the seat next to Manny. They could talk while viewing the parade of pleasure boats heading south to Ponce Inlet and then out to the Atlantic. They both ordered unsweetened ice tea with lemon. Catherine asked for a salad with gator bites. Manny ordered a steak sandwich.

"Where's that wonder dog of yours?" Catherine asked.

"She's at the department being spoiled rotten by Dani. I swear Peaches gets a stomach ache every time Dani tends to her. But they both seem to love watching each other. Actually, Peaches is part of what I want to talk to you about."

"You're not going to tell me you won't let her be honored at the charity auction, are you? Because I won't listen to it."

"No no. Everybody likes to hear about a dog saving the day. No, it's a proposal to honor someone else along with Peaches. Have you heard of Daytona Pete?"

"The man in the news who intercepted the mayday call a few days ago?"

"He's the one. I thought it might be a nice human-interest story to honor him at the auction along with Peaches. He owns a condo on the ocean in Daytona Shores. You should see his living room, Cat. His hobby is talking to people around the world on his ham radio. He often receives signals from passing ships. He can't see them because they're over the horizon, but sometimes they have conversations over his radio. Some of the ships pass regularly and have come to know him. He's also helped a few of them, alerting the coast guard if they were in need of assistance."

"The storm really whipped up in the late afternoon," Catherine said. "Was he looking for a boat in trouble?"

"Not really, but his radio was on. When Pete made contact with this latest boat in distress, he checked with the coast guard to be sure they heard the mayday call. They had, but the officer on duty asked Pete to keep monitoring the situation in case the skipper changed channels. Unfortunately, because of the storm they couldn't find the boat until it turned up the next morning, beached on the shore of New Smyrna."

"I think that's a wonderful idea to give him some recognition. Can I put out a press release on him?"

"Sure. He has a great story. He's an Iraq war vet. Unfortunately, he stepped on a land mine and lost both of his legs. He has artificial limbs but prefers the wheelchair when he's home. He pretty much stays in his condo. Oh, he also plays the horses. I mean he *really* plays the horses. He calls his living room, his OTBP, or for us laymen, his off-track betting parlor."

"Sounds like an interesting man," Catherine said. "What arrangements do you want me to make? A limo to pick him up?"

"No, I think Peaches and I will bring him over. Turns out Peaches really likes the guy. I'll send you an email this afternoon with a write-up for the press. Cat," Manny said, leaning over, and taking her hand in his, "thank you for helping me out. I know I can always count on you."

"Manny, it's really the other way around. Honoring a man like Daytona Pete will bring people to the auction, and then the auction will be a huge success raising money for the charities it supports. So you see, you're helping me." She leaned over and gave him a friendly kiss on the cheek.

Manny tried to ignore the warm spot that remained where her lips had touched his cheek. "Tell me, what's going on with you these days besides work, work, and more work?" he said, polishing off his steak sandwich.

"I may have a new project. Actually, I learned about this new possibility the morning I caught the news story about the beached yacht. I was on my way out the door to the House of Beads. Tillie, you remember her, don't you? You interviewed her after Russell's wife died in the shop."

"Yes, a very pleasant woman," Manny said, taking a sip of water to wash down the last of his lunch now that he had control of the flutters in his stomach.

"Anyway, she called me because the shop adjacent to hers is vacant, and she wanted my thoughts about expanding into the space. She had the key so we went in for a look-see. We tossed a few ideas around, and one of my suggestions was to incorporate a cyber café with her bead business. Her weekend traffic is very heavy but a bit lighter during the week."

"Sounds interesting."

"It does, doesn't it? A cyber café, especially for salespeople and students, could boost her income during the week. She's going to mull over the idea as well as some others we had. I also have to check on how to set up the networking and Wi-Fi so they perform at the highest speed possible, as well as how to charge users, a business model, if you will. I've done schematics with networks for various buildings but not the nuts and bolts."

"It's an ambitious project. Daytona Pete might be able to help you with your so called nuts and bolts. His background is in electronics. Do you want me to ask him if he would be interested in the project? To be honest with you, if he said yes, you would be doing him a big favor. He wouldn't look at it that way to start, but I'd like to see him get a life, so to speak, rather than sitting in his condo all day. Mind you, he's very busy with his OTB," Manny said chuckling, "but I think it would be good for him to be with people once in a while."

"Oh, Manny, would you ask him? He could be perfect. At least, I'd be able to get some idea of what I'm getting into and work up some pricing."

"What do you mean, what you're getting into?"

"Tillie doesn't have the capital to start a totally new business. I told her I was looking for a project, a venture capital investment. I think this idea looks like it could be a very interesting place to start."

Chapter 15

— • • • —

"WELCOME TO CHANNEL 13 news at noon.

"We have breaking news out of Edgewater, Florida. A fisherman found two male bodies washed up on the beach.

A member of the Edgewater Police Department told Channel 13 that the bodies had no identification on them. They've been transported to the Volusia County morgue in Daytona Beach to determine cause of death, but the guess is they drowned, perhaps during our recent storm. We will keep you updated as more information becomes available.

Now back to the traffic report."

Chapter 16

— • • • —

THE DAY WAS MILD, but Manny was agitated. He decided to make a run to the morgue to talk to Sam about the two bodies found that morning on the Edgewater shoreline.

"Sam, what have you got for me on those two John Does?" Manny asked barging into Sam's laboratory. "How long do you think they've been in the water?"

"And ga-day to you, too," Sam responded in his best Aussie accent. "It's hard to say. At least several days. They are white males, fairly young, late twenties maybe. They carried no identification of any kind on their bodies. They both drowned. Could be they were fishing and got caught in that storm."

"Can Dani get pictures of their faces, or are they too messed up?"

"One of them would be impossible, but she might get a likeness from the other."

"Okay. She'll drive over a little later. Sam, do you think they could have any relationship with our John Doe on the Molly C?"

"I don't see any connection. These two are quite a bit younger than John Doe. Strange that nobody has come forward inquiring about any of these men."

Manny left the morgue and drove back to the department. He charged up to the bullpen, Peaches following close on his heels. Spotting her pillow next to her master's desk, she circled on top a couple of times, then nestled down and fell asleep. Dani was still in her lab. Fred and George entered the bullpen a few minutes after Manny and sat down at their desks. George gave Dani a quick heads up on the intercom, alerting her that Manny was ready for their team meeting. She darted back to the bullpen with a half-full cup of Dunkin French Vanilla coffee in her hand. She almost collided with Hutch coming around the corner with his own cup of java.

"Hutch, nice of you to join us," Manny said a slight edge to his voice. "We'll bring you up-to-date with what we know so far. We have two more John Does. Sam's report will be on my desk tomorrow. Only thing of interest is there were no IDs on the bodies, and they were found south about a half mile from where the Molly C was beached. There may or may not be a tie in with the boat case. Probably not," Manny reported. "Dani, when we finish, please go over to the morgue and see Sam. He thinks you might get a picture of the face of one of the two new John Does. Let's call them Doe two and Doe three. Have you been able to find anything on the origin of the boat?"

"Not a thing," Dani said. "It may have come from an island in the Caribbean, somewhere outside of the States. I sent an email to the Miami Police Chief, as well as Jacksonville, with pictures of the Molly C. Given the storm was on all the airwaves, I'm wondering if they topped off their fuel tanks before heading out, either from Jacksonville going south or from Miami heading north. Maybe the nexus of events happened to be Ponce Inlet. I also included a picture of John Doe one, although he looks pretty bad. Maybe one of the Chief's detectives can find somebody who saw the boat. After I get a picture of our new Doe, I'll ship it off to see if, by any chance, there is a connection."

"Good work," Manny said. "Hutch is in charge of the terrorist angle—the cocaine and ricin investigation along with John Doe one. He'll also represent the Drug Enforcement Administration. We'll assist, especially with the murdered man. Dani, please help him any way you can. I'm sure he'll want the information from the Miami and Jacksonville departments if they come up with something. We'll stay on John Does two and three for now. Did you include a picture of the tattoo on Doe one with your emails?"

"Yep. Hutch, I'll get you a copy as soon as we finish," she said.

"I'll need samples of the two powders you found," Hutch said. "I'm heading back to Washington in the morning, and I want to get them to our lab ASAP. As soon as I assign my cases to another agent, I'll be back. Definitely by the day of the auction."

"Fred, any hitches with the round-the-clock stakeout at the marina?" Manny asked. "With the beaching of the Molly C all over the news, I'm sure the owner of the powder is trying to determine if we found it."

"There's a 24/7 watch," Fred replied. "One officer is on the boat at all times, very visible. I told Ted Adams the security detail is standard procedure for a crime scene."

"Hutch and I met with Daytona Pete yesterday morning," Manny said, "about a plan to get some publicity on the boat and his role in the intercepted mayday call. He went along with it as long as it didn't interfere with his Kentucky Derby handicapping. It's a wonder that guy has any money, although he swears he wins more than he loses."

Manny unwrapped a Nicorette, popping it in his mouth. "I had lunch with Catherine Hainsworth today to see if she would include an award for Pete at the charity auction, along with my friend Peaches here." At the sound of her name, Peaches responded with a thump of her tail and went back to sleep.

Hutch looked up at Manny with the news he had met with Catherine. He tried to tamp down a skip in his heart when he heard her name.

"She was delighted and thought the publicity would actually help the auction raise more money," Manny said. "Remember, nobody outside our team will know all the facets of the investigation. Everything is on a need-to-know basis, including our undercover officers. Dani, get the backpacks and the replacement bricks ready. Let's schedule the media shoot for three days from now at ten in the morning. I'll check with Pete to make sure he's good with the plan and the timing. We certainly don't want to get too close to Derby day. Hutch, are you okay with Dani's plan to replace the bricks and the metal box with flour?"

"Yes," Hutch said. "We should remove the stash from the boat as quickly as possible. The owners are probably thinking up all kinds of cockamamie schemes to get it back. The loss of nearly three-million bucks must be putting a crimp in their scheme. If someone is watching, we don't want to tip our hand that we know what's on board. Give me the latest on your plan."

"As we talked about before, we'll stage a photo shoot with Pete, but *without* the media," Manny said. "The five of us—Fred, George, Dani, Pete and I—will arrive at the marina unannounced. We'll make a fuss getting Pete out of the van and over to the yacht to take his picture for the auction award ceremony. While Dani makes a big deal on the ground positioning Pete and Peaches for the photo op, we three guys, sporting backpacks, will sprint up the stairs to the yacht's stateroom and back down after making the switch."

"I figure they could carry twelve bricks apiece," Dani interjected. "They'd only have to make three round trips each. They could ham it up calling to one another to bring a different piece of equipment for additional forensic tests on the blood or whatever."

"The backpacks would be prepped earlier," Manny continued, "each containing the same number of bricks. We make the switch, dropping the cocaine bricks in the van and strapping on an identical bag with flour for the next trip."

"I could even make a trip," Dani said, "indicating that Pete wanted some pictures with his camera. I would be adding to the chaos. After the shoot, I'll stream the video and stills of Pete sitting by the Molly C to the television stations and the *News Journal* to run with the press release for the auction."

"How does it sound to you, Hutch?" Manny asked, patting his breast pocket for another Nicorette.

"I say do it. The sooner the better."

"We have three undercover officers at the marina now working in two shifts as maintenance guys, and one more as a night watchman," George said. "The men applied for jobs that were open and were hired on the spot. Ted Adams is unaware they are undercover officers. When we know exactly the time of Operation Switch, I'll tell the officer at the crime scene that he's relieved while we get more forensics. I'll notify him to return when we're done."

"Let me know when the transfer is completed," Hutch directed. "Dani, if I can have a sample of the ricin, I'll be on my way."

Hutch got up to leave the bullpen, giving Peaches a pat on the head as he left.

Thump. Thump.

Chapter 17

— • • • —

"WHERE HAS THE DAY GONE?" Hutch muttered to himself. He had started to call Catherine several times, but he was always interrupted. It had been several weeks since he'd seen her. He hadn't called during that time trying to keep his distance, but now that he was so close he could no longer fight the desire to see her. He went to his car, turned on the air conditioning, fished his cell phone from his belt, and punched in her number. His heart missed a beat when he heard her voice.

"Hi, Catherine, it's Hutch."

"Hutch, darling. How wonderful to hear from you. Are you calling from Washington?"

"I'm calling about three miles from you. I've been trying to get away all day to ask you to dinner tonight."

"When did you get to town?"

"Late last night and I leave early in the morning unless you say no to dinner. In which case, I'll hop a flight back tonight. However, I hope you say yes."

"I'd love to have dinner with you. Do you want to drop by for a cocktail first?"

"Catherine, dear, that sounds wonderful. I've developed a powerful thirst with all the activities today. Is seven too early?"

"Seven's fine. See you soon."

— • • • —

CATHERINE HUNG UP THE PHONE. The butterflies in her stomach were flying at mach speed. "For heaven's sake, it's only dinner," she said to herself. She flew up her spiral staircase to her dressing room. *Let's see, Hutch will more than likely ask me for a restaurant suggestion,* she thought. *He'll probably be dressed semi-casual, but everything around here is casual, plus or minus. Maybe I'll play it down the middle. This little black number can go anywhere.*

She removed the dress from its hanger, laid it on the bed, and headed for the shower. *The night is going to be a bit chilly, she thought, rare for us at this time of year, so somewhere inside. I know, the Top of Daytona. Then we can look out over the ocean for at least an hour before it gets dark.*

Catherine found herself humming as she showered and dressed. A spritz of Chanel No. 5 and she was ready. In the kitchen, she placed martini glasses, vodka, and dry vermouth on the wet bar. She tossed together cashews, dried cranberries, and golden raisins to accompany their cocktails. A push of the button on her CD machine and soon the beautiful strains of a Rachmaninoff concerto quietly filled the lower level of the house through speakers wired in each room. Pictures of the few times she had seen Hutch played in her mind—meeting at the charity ball, a couple of dinner dates, and then the frightening episode in Jamaica when he and Manny apprehended the killer of Russell's wife.

The doorbell rang causing a flush to dot her cheeks as she went to greet her visitor. She still wasn't prepared for the impact of seeing him again. His six-foot-six muscular frame filled the doorway—his smile captivating, topped by blue eyes and dark brown hair, slightly mussed up. His waning English accent spoke of his British heritage, unless, of course, he was undercover.

Hutch offered Catherine a nosegay of violets accompanied by a soft kiss on her cheek. Flustered by his gift and kiss, she said, "Please come in Agent Hutchinson. I'm not used to such a gallant man on my doorstep."

Catherine led him to the kitchen. "What would you like to drink, a little wine or maybe something stronger? On the phone, it sounded as if you had a hectic day."

"A martini would be perfect. I see you have the prescribed ingredients to quench my thirst out on the bar. Would you prefer the wine?"

"A martini for me as well, thank you. The violets are so pretty, one of my favorite flowers," Catherine said, putting the violets in a small crystal bowl. "Let's have our drinks in the library, and then you must tell me what brings you to our fair city. Another case?"

Catherine's library was the epitome of coziness. Windows lined one wall, punctuated with a French door, inviting guests out to her beautiful garden. Cherry bookcases, six-feet tall, faced the windows. Above the bookcases hung pictures of all sizes framed in various woods, as well as black, gold and silver. The pictures told her life story. Sitting on top of the bookcases were memorabilia from her youth, several tennis trophies, and treasures from her adult travels. A small television sat on one of the bookshelves. The floor of white tile was enhanced by a large oriental rug to give the room warmth. Two caramel-colored leather recliners faced an overstuffed apple-green velour couch. The room afforded a quiet retreat, a place to read and reflect.

"Catherine, this is a beautiful room. I bet you did the decorating. It has your touch."

"Yes, I did and thank you," she said, smiling as she curled up on the couch. Hutch chose the comfort of her late husband's recliner. "I'm working full time on interior designs as well as some architectural schematics for Stone and Associates."

"Ah, now I *must* invite you to Washington. When I was recruited by Homeland Security, I bought a modest antique townhouse in Georgetown. I love the place and the city. But when I say antique, I mean it needs help. Nothing in my thirty-eight years prepared me for the problems that come with an old house."

"Well, I do go to the District occasionally," Catherine said taking a sip of her martini. "I've been meaning to ask you, do I detect an English accent? Where did it come from?"

God, she's stunning, he thought, curled up on that couch, her blonde hair so soft around her face, and that little black dress following her curves. "I was born in Boston of British parents. Although I don't think I have an accent, others seem to hear it. Mom and Dad sent me abroad to boarding school in London. Because my parents believed, like many Europeans, that children should speak numerous languages, I learned to speak German, French, and Spanish."

"I wish we emphasized more the importance of learning several languages," Catherine said, taking a sip of her cocktail.

"When it was time to pick a career, I wanted this important part of my education to be in the States," Hutch said. "The University of Michigan trained me in law enforcement, but the streets of LA trained me how to survive. That's where Homeland Security found me. I was recruited to work in the illegal immigration and terrorism branch."

Hutch stopped his soliloquy. The couple seemed very comfortable with the silence between them, sipping their drinks and listening to the music in the background.

"Have you ever been married?" she asked. She had noticed his ring finger was bare.

"No. Never have. There was either the wrong girl at the right time or maybe the right girl at the wrong time. My job is not conducive to any kind of involvement—lots of travel, stressful assignments, as well as potential danger," he said finishing his drink.

"I think it's time to get some nourishment into that hulk you call a body, Hutch. Because it's a little chilly, I thought maybe something indoors. Have you been to the Top of Daytona?"

"No, I haven't. Am I dressed for it? I have a tie in the car."

"Perfect—no tie required."

—•••—

Catherine and Hutch chit-chatted on their way to the restaurant as if they had known each other forever. They crossed the causeway over the Halifax River from Port Orange, a long expanse to the beachside.

"No matter how many years I live in Florida," Catherine said, "which is my whole life by the way, I never get tired of this crossing from the mainland to the beach side. Just look at the sailboats and pleasure boats dotting the river."

"You love it here, don't you, Catherine."

"Yes, I do. I swear I love it more each year. I count my blessings every day that I live in such a beautiful place."

Arriving at the restaurant, Hutch turned up the driveway and stopped under the portico. He got out of the car and gave the keys to the valet. Catherine took his hand and guided him to the express elevator, which ran up to the restaurant that crowned the building. When the elevator door opened, Hutch was immediately taken with the view. The Atlantic Ocean seemed to envelop the restaurant from three sides. Catherine requested the maitre d' to seat them in a southeast corner window if possible. The west wall blocked the setting sun so the dinner guests were shielded from the glare.

"What a spectacular view. Thank you, Catherine."

"I'm afraid I did nothing. This scene was created by Mother Nature and the interior design by Stone and Associates," she said, slowly waving her hand from one end of the ocean to the other and back again to the interior.

"Would you like some wine with dinner, my dear?" Hutch asked. Again he couldn't take his eyes off her. The soft light of early evening, coupled with the flicker of the table's candle, surrounded Catherine with a glow so soft he was afraid she would evaporate.

"A glass of wine would be very nice. The fish is particularly good here, but I imagine a steak is more what you have in mind," she said, looking up into his eyes. "They're known here for their steak au poivre, so I believe that is what I'll order."

"Steak it is." Hutch signaled the waiter and ordered a bottle of their bin twenty-five, a hearty red wine from Spain.

The waiter returned shortly with the wine. Removing the cork, he poured a taste into Hutch's goblet. After Hutch accepted the rich, dark red liquid, the waiter filled Catherine's glass and then topped off Hutch's glass as well.

"Are you ready to order, sir?" the waiter asked, his pen and pad ready to record their selections.

Hutch ordered dinner for Catherine and himself. If he wasn't sure of something, he guessed and looked at her questioningly to see if he was right or if she wanted to change the selection. She agreed with all of his choices.

After the waiter retreated, Hutch lifted his glass to hers and tapped it gently. "Here's to a most beautiful woman. Thank you for accepting my invitation."

For a moment they were both lost in the magic that wrapped around them. Catherine finally broke away and looked at the panorama of the ocean, but she didn't speak.

Turning back to him, she asked, "Such a quick trip. You didn't say if it was business or pleasure?"

"Manny asked me to come down to check on a few issues from the last case, and I wanted to see a buddy of mine, William Peterson. I guess he's known around here as Daytona Pete."

"My goodness, what a small world. We, that is the charity auction is going to honor Daytona Pete for his good work. He lives down the way. You can almost see his condo from here. He intercepted a mayday call and alerted the coast guard. But he has helped more than a few boaters when they didn't heed the warnings of choppy seas. I guess he talks to passing ships as well over his ham radio. Did he mention he was going to be an honoree?"

"Yes, he did. But he didn't say it was at the charity auction, or I would have known you would be involved." Looking out at the ocean, he thought, *I have to be careful what I say, so I don't get her involved in the case.*

"He and Peaches are going to make it a very special event, and I believe they will help us raise more money. They both have a lovely story. Do you see that lighthouse south of here?" Catherine asked, pointing out the window. "It's not far from where Daytona Pete lives."

"Yes, I do," Hutch answered. This is great, he thought, I've got a bird's eye view of the whole area.

Dinner arrived and more wine was poured. The two enjoyed each other's company, but then the after-dinner espresso signaled that the evening was coming to an end.

"Look, do you see the sweep of the lighthouse beam way over there?" she asked, looking south out of the window. "That's the Ponce Inlet lighthouse I pointed out to you earlier."

Hutch turned to the window and caught the beam as it swung around. "Yes, I do."

"The beached boat, the one that's been in the news, was near the point, Ponce Inlet, where you see the beam of light. They found a dead man on board. Shot in the head. According to the news, the authorities don't know who he is, or where the boat came from. It was freed from the beach, quite a sight, I tell you, with all the equipment that was needed. She was then towed to a marina here in Daytona Beach on the Halifax River. We can't see the marina because it's behind us."

"Sounds like big news with the body and all."

It was now dark and the windows became mirrors, reflecting the dining room with a few guests lingering over their after dinner drinks in the soft candlelight. Catherine and Hutch finished their coffee and reluctantly retraced their steps to the car. Hutch helped her into the rented Lincoln and started the drive to her house.

The night was crisp. Stars punctuated the sky, and the lights on either side of the causeway over the Halifax twinkled brightly, their images skipping over the gentle current of the river. Hutch pulled into her driveway and turned off the ignition. Sitting in silence for a moment, he reached for her hand, turned it over and kissed her palm. *Damn, this woman does something to me,* he thought.

Getting out of the car, he walked around and opened her door. Strolling up to the entrance of her house, Hutch said, "I wish I didn't have to return to DC so quickly. It's been a wonderful evening, Catherine."

"I enjoyed it, too. Any chance you might come down when your friend Daytona Pete is honored?"

He couldn't tell her that he would definitely be down for fear of jeopardizing the operation, but he could fudge it a little. "Let's just say I'll see what I can do."

He touched her hair and then put both hands on either side of her face. "You are a special woman, Catherine." He touched his lips softly to hers, and she returned the sweet warmth. He opened her door. She stepped inside and turned back to face him. "Thank you again, Agent Hutchinson," she whispered.

He returned to his car and drove out into the night.

Chapter 18

— • • • —

CATHERINE, DRIVING ON AUTOPILOT, was still in somewhat of a trance after her dinner date with Hutch the night before. She had fallen asleep dreaming of their candlelight dinner and the sweet kiss he gave her when he said goodnight on her doorstep. A kiss that promised he would be seeing her again.

Catherine pulled into the parking lot in front of the bead shop. She and Tillie had agreed to meet to discuss their ideas for expansion.

Tillie was restocking some fresh water pearls when Catherine entered the shop. "Help yourself to coffee, hon. It's a new brew of French roast with cinnamon. Smells nice, don't you think?" Tillie said. "I'll just be a couple of minutes."

Catherine helped herself to the coffee, adding a thimble of cream. "Can I take the key? I'd like to get some measurements," Catherine asked, juggling her large tote containing a laser measuring tool, a construction calculator, notes to discuss with Tillie, and her fresh cup of coffee.

"Sure. The key is on the counter. I'll be right over."

Catherine let herself into the adjacent shop and set her things on the floor in front of the bay window. Retrieving the notepad and the measuring tool, she beamed the device from the corner of one wall to the next, noting the results on her pad. She punched the measurements into her calculator and immediately had the square footage. Tillie soon joined her, a mug of coffee in hand.

"I brought over a couple of folding chairs for us this morning and a table," Tillie said, unfolding the chairs.

"Thanks, Tillie. The table will make things easier. Great coffee by the way. What did you find out about the building? Is it for sale or rent?" Catherine asked.

"None of the buildings in the plaza are for sale. The rent is the same as mine. Also, the plaza manager talked to the corporate owner.

He liked the idea of my expanding because he felt my shop was a drawing card. When I mentioned our idea about a cyber café, he really got excited, and said he would hold it for one month."

"A month works. We should have a good idea of cost and a working draft of a business plan by then," Catherine said, sitting down on one of the chairs and taking a sip of coffee. "Have you had any other thoughts for the space?"

"Only one, very incidental, but playing a little on your idea of a cyber café. I really don't want to be in the coffee-making business, and I detest the smell of stale, burned coffee on a hot plate. Yet, coffee is a nice amenity for the customers. My thought was that every café customer with a purchase over five dollars would receive a coupon for a free cup of coffee from the Coffee Hut on the other side of my bead shop."

"I think that would be a very nice touch and very smart. Customers love to receive something extra for their money," Catherine said. She set her cup down, and pulled out a portfolio holding some pictures as well as typed pages.

"Tillie, let me paint a scene for you. Are you familiar with Van Gogh's café terrace works?"

"Yes. Strong colors—yellows, oranges, deep blues," Tillie replied.

"Okay, keep those colors in mind, but now picture a French farmhouse with several out buildings—same strong yellows and oranges from the house as well as fields of wheat. The skyline is a lovely blue, rather like the wings of a Blue Jay. There are wispy white clouds in the blue sky and even a pale silvery half moon in the distance. The scene you're looking at would be painted as a mural on your walls. The mural surrounds a patio—the cyber café. The patio floor is paved with large terracotta stones, the ceiling painted as the blue sky with the clouds. Indirect lighting washes the walls bringing them to life in vivid colors."

"I see it. I see it. What will the customers sit on?"

"There is a raised deck in the far corner, not large, but big enough to accommodate two love seats and a couple of comfortable chairs, all upholstered in terracotta leather—an inviting spot to chat with a friend or use the Wi-Fi on their laptop. It would serve as a gathering place, especially in the beginning while we create awareness of the café. Once we get up to speed, we can reconfigure the deck with more room for paying customers. On the main floor would be two kiosks with four stations—monitors, keyboards, mouse—connected to one computer located in the back room. The computer will serve as the connection to the Internet."

"Excuse me, Catherine, but I don't quite see the kiosk concept."

"It's just a fancy word for workstation—a table large enough to accommodate two computer monitors, back to back, four in all. In addition to the cabled kiosk systems, the whole space will be a hot spot for wireless connections, Wi-Fi. I've found a few companies who cater to cyber cafes. They will provide us with a turnkey operation and handle all hardware problems, software upgrades, and customer support."

"Wow, you've done a lot of research. I like it, I like it," Tillie said, her face beaming as further ideas rushed through her mind.

"There is one other important consideration," Catherine said. "We want to incorporate your beads into the new space so it feels as if the two areas flow together. I thought maybe a series of shadow boxes with a Van Gogh print in each. Pieces of jewelry, or strands of beads, in colors represented in the print could hang inside the box. The box would have a locked glass door on the front with a description of the beads, or perhaps jewelry offered for sale. Here are a couple of printouts with several of Van Gogh's flower paintings to give you an idea for color."

"Catherine, I love it. What do we do next? Remember, I don't have funds for such an ambitious undertaking."

"If we go ahead, I'll be your backer. I won't see a dime until you start to make a profit. Once the café is in the black, then a percentage would go to your venture capitalist—that would be me," Catherine said with a smile. "We'll have to draw up the papers with a lawyer so we both know and, more important, agree on the terms and conditions. I also want to be sure the guts of the operation, the kiosks, are set up properly and provide the service we envision. I was talking to Manny the other day, you know, Captain Salinas?"

"Oh yes, that very nice police officer."

"I told him just a little of the possible project, and that I was concerned about the operation of the computers. He suggested we talk to Daytona Pete."

"*The* Daytona Pete who intercepted the mayday call?"

"The very one. He's an electronics and computer guru. He stepped on a land mine while on a patrol in Iraq, and, as a result, he lost both legs. I understand he does have artificial limbs, but he mostly chooses to use his wheelchair. Anyway, Manny thought, this project might get him out of his condo and give him an opportunity to be with people a little more. We're honoring him at the charity auction, and I'll ask him about it. If he says he's interested, I'll set up a meeting here with you and me."

"Catherine, it all sounds beyond my wildest dreams. I just hope you understand I only know my little piece of the world—beads. I wouldn't have the foggiest notion of where to begin to pull off an idea such as you've outlined," Tillie said.

"That, my dear, is why you need a partner. Don't forget you will be giving me an opportunity to become a venture capitalist," Catherine said, her eyes dancing merrily.

"Here's to capitalism," Tillie said, touching her coffee mug to Catherine's cup.

Chapter 19

— • • • —

"WE GOT A HIT," Dani called out.

The team looked up, snapping to attention. Peaches jumped up, her tail wagging in anticipation.

"A marina fuel attendant in Miami remembered the Molly C filling up the day of the storm," Dani said, her eyes wide with excitement. "Officer Bob Dix from the Miami Police Department just sent me an email."

"Fred, you and George get the information from Dani and get your asses down to Miami," Manny said. "If he stopped for fuel, maybe he went ashore for supplies. Keep me posted."

"Dani, we need the pictures you have of John Doe one and two, and a picture of the stern of the Molly C that shows her name," Fred said. "Send them to our cell phones and make a couple prints of each. We may want to show them around. And please get in touch with Dix. Tell him we're on our way to the marina. Ask him to meet us there, if possible."

"Don't forget, guys, Operation Switch with Pete is set for eight o'clock tomorrow morning," Manny reminded them. "So, don't get any ideas about staying in Miami overnight."

— • • • —

AFTER GETTING THE PICTURES from Dani, Fred and George jumped into a marked squad car, figuring they would make better time if other drivers got out of their way. They wouldn't use the siren, but they might turn on the flashing lights from time to time. The marina was located a little north of Miami, a good two-hundred-fifty miles away. They estimated it would take them about four hours to get there, if they were lucky. George radioed the Miami officer who found the marina with their estimated time of arrival. Dix told George he would meet him at the marina in the event he could be of further help. Later

George talked with Dix again, telling him they were fifteen minutes out. Thanks to Fred's fancy driving, they made the trip in less than four hours.

Bob Dix, in uniform, was parked in front of the marina entrance when they arrived. He was standing next to a thirty-something man wearing white overalls with the insignia Marina del Sol on it.

All of them shook hands and introduced themselves to the marina attendant.

"Let's go over to that table in the side yard," Fred said. "We'll have more privacy there."

Officer Dix obviously came prepared, pulling out four ice-cold water bottles from a cooler in his squad car and joined the three at the table.

"Tell us what happened the morning of the storm," Fred said to the attendant. "First, let me show you our John Doe and the boat." Fred pulled on the Velcro to open the pocket on his pant leg and retrieved the three pictures. "Do you recognize this man? He's a little battered so take your time." Fred showed the attendant John Doe two.

"No. I don't recognize him. You're right, he looks bad."

"Bodies in the morgue aren't very pretty. How about this man?" Fred showed him the picture of John Doe one.

"Yes, I recognize this man even banged up. This is the man who stopped for fuel in the Molly C. I remember the boat's name because my niece's name is Molly. I thought it was a really great name for a boat. He acted like he owned her. After Officer Dix asked me about the Molly C, I talked to our cashier and asked her to pull the receipts from that morning. Unfortunately, he paid cash, so I can't give you his name."

"Did he get off the boat? Leave the marina for anything?" George asked.

"Yes. He was in a big hurry. He told me to fill it up fast, that he was heading north and wanted to beat the storm. Then he told me he was going to Catfish Heaven. That's a restaurant across the street. He said he was meeting someone and would be right back. He told me the boat better be ready when he returned. He wasn't very nice, but then I just attributed his behavior to nervousness, what with the storm coming and all."

"Were you the only one pumping fuel that morning?" Fred asked.

"No. That guy over there pumps, too," he said pointing toward the docks. "He's just a kid, but the manager lets him help out when it gets busy."

"I'd like to take that receipt," George said.

"No problem," the attendant replied, handing George the slip of paper.

Even though several hands had touched it, George still pulled on his latex gloves, took the receipt, and put it in a small brown paper bag. If there were any prints of interest, they wouldn't be compromised from a sweaty plastic pouch.

"Fred, let's grab something to eat at Catfish Heaven," George said. "Want to come with us, Bob?"

"Sure, I have time," Dix replied.

"Sounds good to me," Fred said and turned back to the attendant. "Thanks for your help. If you think of anything else, here's my card. We may check back with you later."

Both Officer Dix and Fred headed across the street with George. The restaurant was a typical fast-food joint on the beach—bright colors, loud music, and very casual dress. Customers rarely ate there, preferring take-out, but there was a lunch counter and a few tables. The jukebox was playing a Hannah Montana CD.

The three men settled themselves on the counter stools and pretended they were looking at the menu. All three were giving the once over to the customers eating at the tables. No one else sat at the counter.

The counter waitress, scrubbed clean and dressed in a pink-pinafore apron over a white T-shirt and white, very short shorts, walked over to them with a radiant smile that only a sweet young girl would flash.

"What can I get for you guys?" she said, looking at the handsome young officer Dix.

"A chocolate shake for me," said Fred.

"Make that two," said George

"How about three?" said Dix.

"You guys are putting me on," the girl said laughing.

"No, we're not," they replied in unison, showing wide smiles.

The pink pinafore retreated and shook up three chocolate shakes, topped with whipped cream and a cherry.

"There you are. Three of my shake specials," she said, placing a tall frothy drink in front of each of the men.

"Miss, I wonder if you could tell me if you recognize this man," Fred asked, again retrieving John Doe one.

"Oooh, he doesn't look too good," she said with a grimace. "He does look familiar, but that hole in his head kinda messes me up."

"How about this one?" Fred showed her John Doe two, one of the bodies pulled from the marsh in Edgewater.

"Oh, yes, I'll never forget him. He was sitting with a friend right over there at that table, very peaceable like. Then all of a sudden he jumped up, raced over to me, and demanded his bill. I was very busy that morning so I had to find the darn thing. He kept telling me to hurry because he had to catch up with his friend, which, of course, only made me more nervous."

"What did his friend do?" George asked.

"He had already gone out the door. Finally, because I couldn't find it, he just threw a five dollar bill at me and raced out after his friend running down to the marina. I thought, good riddance and I hope I never saw him again. Gee, I wonder what happened to him, coming up dead and all. Wait a minute. Let me see that first picture again, the guy with the hole in the head."

Fred again handed her the picture of Doe one.

"Um, yes sir. He's the one who came in, looked around, and then sat with another guy. Their table was next to the table of the man in the first picture you showed me. I remember now because when he came rushing in, he looked a little crazy. His eyes, ya know. He only sat down for a minute. I went over and asked him if he'd like a cup of coffee, and he told me to beat it. I think he was the man. No one seemed to be in a good mood that morning. Probably because of the storm coming, ya know. People round here go a little crazy when bad weather rolls in."

Fred and George stood up with their shakes. They thanked Officer Dix for his help and left him under the gaze of Miss Pinafore. Exiting Catfish Heaven, they headed to their squad car in front of the marina.

"Let's talk to that kid pumping fuel before we leave," George said.

They passed their squad car and continued down to the pumping station. The young man was busy filling up the tank on a small twin-engine motorboat, so the two detectives took a seat nearby on a weather-beaten plank bench and sipped their shakes.

When the kid finished with his customer, George waved to him as he and Fred strolled down the short gangplank.

"Hi," Fred said, showing his badge to the boy. "We're trying to find somebody, and it's possible you saw him about a week ago." Fred retrieved John Doe two and showed him the picture.

"Oh ya, a really scary man. He demanded I fill his tank for him and his friend. He said he had to catch up with a boat that just left. He made me really nervous. I overheard one of them say that it could be big. He almost grabbed the nozzle out of my hand to fill it himself, but I told him that my father instructed me to never let the customer take the nozzle."

"Do you remember how he paid?" George asked.

"Sure I do. He gave me a credit card. I remember because it was only the second one I had written up so I was slow, which only made him madder."

"The boat that had just left, the one they wanted to catch, do you remember anything about it?"

"No, I was too busy trying to help the scary man so he would leave."

"Does this look like the boat?" George asked, showing him the picture of the stern with the name Molly C."

"Hey, it could be. But as I said, I just wanted the guys to leave me alone so I wasn't looking around if you know what I mean."

"Do you think you would recognize their charge slip if your cashier pulled the credit receipts for that day?"

"Maybe. I had a lot of customers that morning. That was the day of the storm you know. Everybody was getting their boat ready in case they had to make a run for it."

Chapter 20

— • • • —

BURNING UP INTERSTATE 95, Fred and George reached Daytona Beach late in the afternoon. They parked the car outside the department and raced up to the bullpen. "Hey, Dani," Fred called out.

"What's got you two all fired up?" Dani asked, peeking out the door of her lab.

"Here's a lead, a credit slip on our John Doe two. Nobody at the marina where the Molly C bought fuel could put Doe two and three with Doe one, but they were all there at the same time, same marina, and same restaurant. A young guy pumping fuel said that Doe two and his friend were in a big hurry to follow a boat that had just pulled out of the marina. The boat Doe two wanted to follow could have been the Molly C. Name on the slip is Carl Brown. By the way, Officer Dix was very helpful. We can use him on this case in Miami."

"I'm on it," Dani said. Her fingers started flying over the keyboard. "There's a Carl Brown in Ft. Lauderdale and one in Miami. Let me pull up the driver's license screen." No one budged from the bullpen. They knew how magical Dani could be when she was playing her keyboard.

"Got it," Dani said, her eyes riveted on her monitor. "Carl Brown in Ft. Lauderdale is seventy-two and bald. Miami Brown is thirty-one and definitely resembles Doe two." Dani hit the print button and took a swig from her coffee mug. The printer sprang to life spitting out the photo ID of Carl Brown, Miami. A match.

"I'll call Dix and ask him to pay Brown's home a visit," George said. "We forwarded the pictures to his cell phone when we were down there with him."

"I'll call Hutch to see if his department can find a registration for the Molly C on one of the Caribbean islands close enough to Miami that they might pull in for fuel," Fred said. "I'll also check to see if he's made any progress on the origin of the ricin. If it's home grown, they won't be able to trace it unless samples from the same batch are in their databank."

— •••—

EARLY THE NEXT day Officer Dix called George. "Hang on, Dix, let me put you on the speaker. Detective Watson, you met him yesterday, is here as well as our Captain Manny Salinas and Sergeant Dani Trotter."

"Sounds good," Dix said through the scratchy speaker. "Carl Brown shares an apartment with Joe Sterling. A neighbor said she hasn't seen either one of them for a couple of weeks. Hey, you guys really owe me for this next one," Dix said.

"And why is that?" George asked.

"The neighbor ID'd your Doe two, and I'm sending you a picture of his friend, Sterling. Maybe you can pick out some distinguishing marks on his face. The woman also said the two guys, while friendly with each other, were not very nice to their neighbors. Another neighbor volunteered that the two owned a small fishing boat. And, get this, they only worked enough to pay the rent and buy food and gas. The manager of the apartment building let me into their place. What a mess. Now, this will really cost you. I'm sending you fingerprints of the two. One more thing. No one recognized your picture of Doe one, and they never heard the name John Anderson."

"Yup, you definitely deserve a steak dinner at your favorite restaurant," George said. "Only problem is our Captain is very stingy on bonuses."

"Screw you, George," Dix chuckled.

— •••—

FRED WAS ABLE to access the fingerprints Dix had referenced from the police database in Tallahassee. He called the morgue and gave the access code to Sam, who said he'd call Fred back as soon as he knew if there was a match with either of the bodies.

With everyone working on tasks Manny had assigned them, the bullpen was quiet. Peaches got up and stretched both her front and back ends. She then nudged Manny's elbow. "Time to check the squirrels, eh girl?" he asked. That was Manny's code to Peaches whenever she had to go do her business.

The two went out into the department's yard ringed with palms and winter oak trees. The latter was a favorite hangout for the squirrels. Peaches knew it, and the squirrels knew it. The squirrels also knew they could drive the dog crazy as they scampered up the trees, jumping from limb to limb. Fifteen minutes later Manny and Peaches returned to Dani's smiling face.

"Sam called. We have a match. We have a match on both men, Doe two and three," Dani said, continuing to grin.

"I did a background on each of them, Brown and Sterling," Dani said. "They've been in and out of jail over the last eight years. Their sentences were nothing longer than a few months to a year, all misdemeanors in the Miami area. However, there was a .38 special registered in Carl Brown's name."

"Okay, now we're getting somewhere," Manny said, writing the names of Brown and Sterling on the case board. "Two options," he said, hitting the board's save button. "They knew Doe one and were in on the plan, or two, they overheard Doe one talking to his contact in the restaurant. Maybe he said the word drugs, or money, or whatever. They decided they could take the guy—Doe one and the boat. Let's say its option two. Somewhere around Ponce Inlet, they jumped John Anderson."

"Okay," George said, "and they tied their fishing boat to the Molly C, or it drifted away when they boarded the yacht because of the waves. In any event, that could explain the rope you recovered from the stern."

"Makes sense." Manny continued, pacing around the bullpen. "So, they succeeded in hijacking the boat after the mayday call, or they had Anderson at gunpoint when he called. They kill Doe one. Fred, call Sam about the .38 when we're finished here. Ask him if the bullet hole in Doe one could have come from a .38. Anyway, with the intensity of the storm, their boat snaps the line and drifts off. Doe two and three are washed overboard, but Doe one gets caught in the lines wrapped around the boat cleat. Doe one, the Molly C, Brown and Sterling were all found within spitting distance of each other. My guess is that option two is what went down. The one piece we're missing from Brown and Sterling is their boat."

"The kid at the marina thought the name on the stern was Big Fish," Fred said. "He definitely remembers the word Fish."

"I'm on it," Dani said before Manny could get the words out of his mouth, her fingers again flying over the keyboard. She paused to sip her coffee when a screen took more than two seconds to load on her monitor.

"George, can you call the Melbourne Chief?" Dani asked, taking no time to look up. "See if they have anything. I'm getting people who looked for boats yanked from their moorings during the storm. So far no names with the word Fish. Doe two and three aren't going to be putting out any can-you-find-my-boat requests. I'll start checking boat registrations in Miami with the word Fish in the name. I'll work as fast as I can, but I have to leave in thirty minutes to pick up Pete for the photo shoot."

While Dani continued to search, George called the Melbourne Police Department, located a hundred-seventy-three miles north of Miami and ninety-one miles south of Daytona Beach. He was transferred to a clerk who maintained a database on the boats coming ashore during and after the storm. She said she'd call him back.

—•••—

WITH HIS TEAM hunkered down over their computers, Manny called Pete to confirm that Dani would pick him up soon. He also left a message for Hutch to call, that there was new information. Manny and Peaches then left for Pelican Bay Marina.

Ted saw Manny drive up and quickly stepped outside to greet his visitor. "Hi, Captain. Any information on my guest, the Molly C?"

"Not yet. I thought I'd check to see if you had any calls regarding her," Manny said. He took note of the new maintenance man, his undercover officer. All seemed quiet.

"Not a word," Ted replied.

"Okay. I'll just go walk around her. We're going to take some pictures, and then I'll be leaving. By the way, are you going to the charity auction Friday night?"

"I wouldn't miss it, especially since your dog and Daytona Pete are going to be honored."

Peaches had been romping in the boat yard, but at the sound of her name came back and sat next to her master. "I don't know about this honoring stuff. She already lives like a princess."

Peaches thumped her tail on the driveway, looking up at Manny. The two strolled off to where the Molly C was berthed. Again, all was quiet. Ted had sent the new maintenance guy over to assist Manny if he wanted anything.

Tony Sullivan, Ted's new guy, and Manny's undercover officer, followed Manny to the boat. "Hi, Captain," Sullivan said.

"Hello, yourself," Manny said. "How's everything going here? Anything unusual?" he asked as he pointed to a phantom spot on the stern of the Molly C, which was at the back of the storage bay, out of sight of any prying eyes.

"Nothing. I don't know about the other shifts, but nothing's going on here during the day with this baby."

"Keep your eyes and ears open," Manny said, "but right now I'd like you to finish your shift back at the department. Fred, George, and Dani are due here soon to take some pictures for an upcoming news story. One more thing, we found a large stash of drugs on board. The other undercover officers on your team are being told as well. You are not to say anything to each other, or anyone else. Got that?"

"Yes, sir."

Chapter 21

—•••—

"THIS IS CHANNEL 13 with news from your community.

The annual Daytona Beach Chamber of Commerce Charity Auction will be held one week from this Friday at the Hilton Hotel. The event will also feature a silent auction. I'm told there will be spectacular treasures available to the highest bidder.

This year's auction, however, is going to be a little different, even more special. The community is honoring two people, or rather one person, an Iraq war veteran, and a dog.

We've all been following the story of the stranded yacht on the shores of New Smyrna Beach. The man, who intercepted the mayday call from the boat during the violent thunderstorm a week ago, is going to be honored. His name is William Peterson, better known around town as Daytona Pete.

Daytona Pete frequently talks to passing ships over his ham radio. The veteran has responded to many calls for help, directions, or guidance since taking up residency in Daytona Shores. Channel 13 has obtained this picture of Daytona Pete, seen here in front of the Molly C.

The honored dog is a black Lab named Peaches, shown sitting next to Daytona Pete. Her owner is Captain Manny Salinas of the Daytona Beach Police Department. A few months ago, Peaches saved a girl's life when she was trapped in the trunk of a car. If Peaches hadn't alerted her master, the girl could have died from dehydration. In the same case, Peaches took out a suspected killer holding a hostage at gunpoint.

So, thank you Daytona Pete and Peaches. We're glad you live and work in our community.

You can meet these two celebrities at the auction. The auction raises money for many worthy charities, including the local chapter of the American Red Cross. Wine and cheese will be served. You are urged to support this gala event."

Chapter 22

— • • • —

TWO DAYS TO THE KENTUCKY DERBY and Pete's condo was vibrating with preparations. Manny and Peaches stood outside of his front door, punched the doorbell a second time.

"Okay, okay. Hold your horses. I'm coming," Pete barked. He pulled the door open ready to unleash some choice words about the parentage of the person who was interrupting him when he saw Peaches.

"Oh, it's you guys. I don't have time to chat, but you can come in. Shut the door, will ya?"

Papers were everywhere. Stacks covered the floor, the chairs, and any spare space on the kitchen counter. The wastebaskets were overflowing if they could be seen at all. A corkboard was propped up on the couch with papers tacked haphazardly. It all meant something to Pete but looked like gibberish to Manny.

Pete barely gave Peaches a scratch behind the ears, so she gave up and went to her favorite spot in front of the sliding glass doors facing the ocean. She soon closed her eyes. The pelicans weren't even flying today.

The printer looked as if it might have a nervous breakdown as it spit out page after page of statistics for the horses running in the Derby. The machine jiggled so violently that it walked to the edge of the tabletop. Wheeling up to the table about to lose its quivering machine, Pete shoved the printer back a foot. A moment later, the machine resumed its journey.

Pete explained to Manny that it was the Daily Racing Form ejecting from the printer. The horses' post positions were announced, which negated his handicapping so far, at least in his eyes. Which gate the horse drew was good news for some and bad news for others. The gate at the far end meant that the horse had more ground to cover than the one coming out of gate one, which was closest to the rail.

His three computer screens were refreshing at an alarming rate. One monitor gave him minute-by-minute updates on the weather forecast for Saturday. Storms were coming from the west and from the Gulf. The weather factored into Pete's handicapping. Some horses didn't do well if mud was thrown in their eyes; others didn't seem to care. The jockeys wore as many as six pairs of goggles if the track was muddy. They kept flipping up pair after pair as each lens mudded over.

The unknown horse in the Derby was Big Brown. He had raced only three times so nobody knew quite how to handicap him. He drew gate twenty—not good, but at least he'd have room to run. There was the filly, Eight Belles. She was getting a lot of hype. The last time a filly won, Genuine Risk, was in 1980. She was just one of three fillies to ever win the Derby. The morning line on Eight Belles didn't give her much of a chance to win.

"Just a minute, Manny," Pete said. "Santiago just updated his blog on Big Brown. Let me print it. I have to have a hard copy to study his handicapping of the race, so I can mark it up with my own analysis."

"This Santiago, he's a favorite of yours?" Manny asked.

"He's the best," Pete said. "Damn, would you look at that—the printer ran out of paper. Just a sec, I have to enter a new print command to my other printer. Shit, now it's jammed." Pete threw his arms in the air. "Maybe it's time to take a break before everything melts down. How about a beer?"

"I'll pass thanks."

"Geez, Manny, it's almost lunchtime. Don't you guys get to wash your food down with something? There's some ham and cheese in the fridge. Would you mind making me a sandwich while I see if I can resuscitate this printer? Make one for yourself, too, and go ahead and tell me why you're here. I'm sure you didn't come over to see my pretty face. However, the pics from the photo shoot were pretty good, if I do say so myself."

"You're right. We need to talk about the arrangements for the auction on Friday," Manny said, getting out the sandwich fixings. "Have you had any weird phone calls?"

"No. I haven't had any *weird* calls. Nobody called or hung up without saying anything. No one lurking in the hall, the elevator, or down below my balcony on the beach. You guys worry too much. Hey, can you come here a minute and hold this door open in the back of my printer? I think I found the culprit. Anyway, Hutch called. He's flying down in the morning and will take me to the auction. He wants you to meet us at the door so he can melt into the crowd. He'll bring me back after the presentation. He's staying overnight and then heading back to Washington."

"That sounds good," Manny said, returning to his lunch task. He cut the sandwiches in half, put them on plates, and placed one next to Pete's elbow. "I'm concerned about your safety after the auction. Using you as bait is risky. Can Peaches stay with you a couple of days?"

"You've got to be kidding. How about her going outside? I don't move too fast you know."

"Okay. At least let me put an alarm button under the arm of your wheelchair. If you get an unwanted visitor, you can give us an alert."

"I suppose that's okay." Pete took a bite out of his sandwich, but his free hand was already back on the keyboard. The printer fired up as he scribbled on a sheet of paper fastened to the clipboard in his lap.

"I'll let myself out," Manny said. When he didn't get a response, he put his empty plate on the counter and gave his thigh a slap. "Come on, Peaches. No point sticking around here."

Chapter 23

—•••—

Chamber of Commerce Charity Auction

RIBBONS OF TABLES filled the Hilton Hotel's Grand Ballroom. All were heavily laden with every kind of treasure imaginable. A bid sheet was placed to the side of each object. At the top of the sheet was the name of the item and item number. Underneath the designated item were two columns—one column for the bidder's number and a second column for the bid amount.

When the guests entered the auction, they were assigned a numbered paddle. The number could be used in the silent auction where the treasures were laid out, as well as in the regular auction with the auctioneer.

The regular auction was to occur in the Hilton's dining room where the tables and chairs were left in place. The only difference in the room's normal layout was a medium-sized platform at one end. Standing on the platform was a podium with a microphone wired to several large speakers hidden in the ceiling of the room. In front of the foot-high staging were four six-foot long tables. They were draped with white cotton tablecloths over royal-blue taffeta skirting. The items donated with the highest value were placed on these tables for viewing.

Catherine hired a renowned Florida auctioneer to handle this part of the sale. Items ranged in value from under a hundred dollars to the most valuable, a solitaire diamond pendant hanging from a delicate gold chain. The value of the piece was estimated to be $10,000. The executor of an estate of a prominent member of the community donated the necklace. The donor's wish was that upon her death her prized diamond be given to charity.

Manny charged Fred and George with the task of setting up the auction security. The detail included a few undercover officers who mingled with the bidders in both the ballroom and the dining room.

Uniformed officers were stationed at all the doors. The message—don't even think of pulling a dirty trick.

The silent auction was slated to run for two hours. By then, Catherine thought they would be ready to sit down in the dining room. The two community awards for Daytona Pete and Peaches would kick off the regular auction after which the bidding would begin.

The two-hour preview of the items to be auctioned was scheduled to begin at five o'clock in the afternoon; the silent bidding would open at six and run until eight o'clock. Then the presentation of awards and the entire auction would be over before ten. During the course of the evening, various wines would be served at two dollars a glass. All money taken in would go to the proceeds for the evening. Catherine had wangled a wonderful deal with a Florida winery. All they asked in return was that a few banners be hung on the walls indicating they donated the wine. Cocktail napkins imprinted with their winery crest and name accompanied each glass. Not to be outdone, the hotel was serving a variety of canapés, all donated to the cause.

Catherine arrived at four to be sure that everything was ready. She found the event coordinator talking to the florist who had donated flower arrangements for the dining-room tables. Anyone who wanted to purchase an arrangement could take it to the cashier with a donation of twenty-five dollars when they left for the evening. The musicians passed carrying their instruments as they made their way to a baby grand piano in the corner of the silent auction ballroom—a harp, violin, and flute.

At five o'clock bidders started to arrive, signed in with the staff, and received a paddle with their number for the evening. The ballroom began to fill up, and Catherine could hear the buzz as the guests began to log in their bids. The hotel wait staff poured the wine when an attendee requested a glass and collected the money.

A man approached Catherine. "Excuse me. Are you Catherine Hainsworth?" the gentleman asked.

"Yes, I am. Can I help you with something?"

"Well, that remains to be seen. My name is Ted Adams. I'm the general manager of the Pelican Bay Marina."

"Oh, Mr. Adams, I'm so glad you could come. I saw your name in the paper. The beached boat, the Molly C, was towed to your marina, I believe."

"Yes, that's me, but please call me, Ted. I was talking a few days ago to Russell Stone of Stone and Associates, Architects and Builders. I'm proposing the addition of a dining room to the marina, and I asked him for his help in the design of the room, the specifications, and the interior decorating. He said he was tied up with a big project, but he suggested I talk to you. He said you work for him. In fact, he sang your praises as though you would be just the answer for my undertaking."

"That was very kind of him, Ted. I would be interested in discussing your ideas, and we could see if I would be the right designer for your project."

"From Stone's recommendation, I'm sure you can help me out. Can you stop by the marina next week? I'll show you some of my sketches, really just back of the envelope ideas, and see what you think. Would Monday early afternoon, about one-thirty, work for you?"

"That would be fine. I look forward to seeing your plans."

—•••—

AT 7:30 CATHERINE, standing off in an alcove overlooking the silent auction, felt a tap on her shoulder. She turned to see who was behind her but she already knew. How could she forget the scent of his cologne?

"Hutch, you didn't tell me you were coming. I didn't hear so I assumed—" She stopped mid-sentence as Hutch gave her a discreet, gentlemanly peck on her cheek, but he was holding her hand tight against his chest.

"I wasn't sure I could make it, but then this guy here kept bugging me to come down for his big evening, so here I am. Do you know William Peterson, otherwise known as Daytona Pete?" Hutch asked releasing her but still locked onto her warm brown eyes.

"No, I haven't had the pleasure, yet," Catherine said, forcing her eyes away from Hutch and down to Pete. He had left his prosthetics at home as planned.

"It's an honor to meet you, Mr. Peterson," she said, shaking his hand.

"Please call me Pete. My handle on my ham radio is Daytona Pete, but for such a beautiful woman as you, it's just plain Pete. Hutch, you've been holding out on me, you devil. How come you never told me you knew this gorgeous person?"

"Because I knew you'd do what you're doing now, make a big fuss."

"I see. It appears to me you've already made a fuss," Pete said, with a twinkle in his eye.

"All right you two, enough already. Pete, I've been looking forward to meeting you," Catherine said. "I believe Manny talked to you about a project I'm considering. He called me a few days ago to tell me you might like to consult on the idea of a cyber café."

"That he did, pretty lady," Pete said, enjoying the attention and particularly the look of amazement on his friend's face.

"I'm sorry I didn't get back to you right away," Catherine said. "This auction all of sudden took every spare minute of my time. How about we meet with Tillie, the bead shop owner, and take a look at the space. I'll email you some thoughts before so you'll have an idea of the scope of the project. Could you meet next week, say Friday morning?"

"I don't see why not. That's still more than a week before the Preakness."

"Pete here doesn't let anything interfere with a big race," Hutch said, trying to get into the conversation.

"I see. I'll have to remember that," Catherine said, with a smile. "Would you like to look at some of the auction items, Pete? You still have some time before we completely embarrass you, telling everyone about your heroics during the storm and recognizing you for all of your community service."

"Nah. Where's my pal, the dog, that's being honored with me?"

Right on cue, a black furry animal muscled her way into the group. She sat in front of Pete and, as was now her custom, put her paw up on his stump.

"You're a regular ham, Peaches, my friend. I'll take your company any day," Pete said, bending over and gently scratching Peaches behind her ears. She returned the favor with a slurp across his cheek and a violent dusting of the floor behind her.

Manny joined the group on the other end of Peaches' leash. "Greetings all," he said, as he placed a quick peck on Catherine's cheek. "You look lovely as ever, Cat."

Hutch watched the exchange, his brow furrowing a bit.

"Manny, it's so good to see you," Catherine said. "Your officers are doing a superb job, and they look so...so, forceful. No one would dare take anything. Now, I hate to leave this group of auspicious gentlemen, but I have to make sure that everything is ready for our honorees. Manny, as planned, I will give you Peaches' plaque." As she said the dog's name, Catherine leaned down and gave the dog a pat on her black silky head. "And then you will introduce Pete and tell a bit of his wonderful story. After that, we'll all clear the stage for the auctioneer."

—•••—

THE EVENING WENT OFF without a hitch. When Manny introduced Daytona Pete, a cheer went up from the crowd and was quickly followed by a standing ovation. Manny embellished the mayday intercept a little, laying out the bait that *perhaps* Daytona Pete would have access to the boat's storage bay, if anyone asked.

The auction proved to be lively, with several people bidding up a particularly valuable item. Halfway through, the auctioneer announced a ten-minute break and many people headed to the wine station, restrooms, or to chat with a friend. Paddle 133 rested in the lap of a man who sat in the back taking in the proceedings. He did not bid. The only time he left his seat was to move closer to Pete, seemingly to take his measure.

After the auction, Catherine saw Manny, Hutch, and Detective Fred Watson huddled with Daytona Pete out in the parking lot. She could see they were having quite an animated conversation. Not wanting to interrupt them, she got into her car and drove home. She was exhausted, but also higher than a kite. The auction broke all records for money raised by any charity event in Daytona Beach.

—•••—

A REPORTER FROM Channel 13 attended the auction as did one from the local paper, *The News Journal*. They left with an updated press release Manny wrote containing all the buzz words he wanted put out over the air and in print. Hopefully the additional publicity, along with more pictures taken at the event, would draw out someone who knew about the boat's cargo or at the very least something about the Molly C's origin.

Hutch saw Catherine drive off. *Damn,* he thought, *I wanted to see her, alone.* Unfortunately, he was the first to stand guard with Pete in the event someone took the bait.

— ••• —

PRIOR TO THE auction, Hutch installed the alert button on Pete's wheelchair. He insisted Pete test it. Within seconds Dani called Hutch on his cell and told him she had received the alert. If no one was present in the bullpen, the alert would go to the front desk sergeant. Hutch also had suggested Pete attend the auction in his wheelchair as part of the decoy scheme to make him look more vulnerable. Pete's blousy shirt and unbuttoned sport coat covered a 9mm Glock pistol in his waistband.

Over the weekend, George, Fred, and another officer, if necessary, would take shifts with Pete at his condo. Fred, excited about watching Pete wager on the Kentucky Derby, volunteered to take the first twenty-four-hour shift from Saturday morning to Sunday morning. George would take the next twenty-four hours. Hutch told Manny he planned to leave for Washington Saturday morning as soon as Fred came on duty. All the lawmen hoped someone would take the bait from the auction's publicity. After the first forty-eight hours, Pete was on his own with his alert button and gun.

"All bases seem to be covered so let's break up this merry band of men and get some shut eye," Manny said. "Good luck on the Derby tomorrow, Pete. Hope you win a bundle."

Pete leaned over giving the *honored* dog a pat on the head and received a lick in the ear in return. Pete and Hutch left the hotel parking lot and headed for the condo and an ice cold beer.

"You didn't get a chance to say goodbye to the pretty lady. I saw her pull out. She looked your way, or was it Manny's way?" Pete murmured.

"Shut up and mind your own business," Hutch growled. "Give a man a plaque for service and he thinks he owns you." Both men smiled congenially as Hutch merged into traffic. Daytona Beach, known for its night life, always seemed to have traffic. Hutch was anxious to get to Pete's condo, grab that beer, and head for the balcony with his cell phone.

—•••—

"CATHERINE, Hutch here. I didn't get to say goodnight to you. You did a terrific job."

"Hutch, darling," Catherine said. "I'm so glad you called, I'm still running on adrenaline and doubt I can sleep a wink. I wish you had told me you were coming."

"I wasn't sure I could get away, but things cleared up at the last minute. Catherine, an idea's been rolling around my brainless head ever since I saw you tonight. You looked gorgeous, by the way. You made this bachelor's heart skip a beat."

"Well, that's good to hear. What's this idea rolling in your head? Did it find a pocket yet?"

"Tell me you play billiards, and I'll throw you over my shoulder and cart you away," Hutch countered jovially. "Yes, the idea found a corner pocket. I'm leaving for Washington tomorrow morning, and I was wondering if you could join me for the weekend. There's a very nice inn a few blocks from my townhouse. I thought I could show you around Georgetown, maybe a little dinner, and dancing. And don't forget, you said you'd give me your thoughts on how I can make my bachelor pad more comfortable. What do you say? Please say yes."

"Agent Hutchinson, you make my head spin. I suppose I could make it," she said. "I'd have to be back early Monday morning to help the staff get a final tally of the receipts from the auction, and I have a meeting with a client at one-thirty. Hutch, I'd have to fly back to Daytona Beach or I'd never make my appointments on time."

"Catherine, my dear, I'll get you back on time, even if I have to commandeer Air Force One. I have a plane ready to pick us up tomorrow morning, and one that will drop you off Monday in time for your meeting. Pete wants me out of his condo tomorrow early because it's Derby day. Nobody messes with Daytona Pete on race day. He and I'll have coffee, finish our visit by 8:30. Would you mind meeting me at the Daytona Beach Airport, say around nine?"

"I'll be there. Thanks a lot, Agent Hutchinson. Flying off to Washington with you in a private plane, just like Cinderella, now I know I won't sleep a wink tonight."

Chapter 24

— • • • —

Race Day - Kentucky Derby

CHURCHILL DOWNS RACE TRACK in Kentucky was the scene of mud, sweat, and flaring nostrils. However, Derby day on the east coast of Florida was quiet and serene. Sipping coffee on Pete's balcony, Hutch was enjoying the peace. A sliver of sun could be seen on the horizon, painting the few cloud skiffs in hues of pink.

Inside Pete's living room, however, was a very different story. Both printers were spitting out page after page of updated statistics. He, as well as those wagering around the world, would use this mountain of information to construct bets on the Derby entries, a field of twenty horses.

Pete's first job was to eliminate some of the field. He didn't want to waste any money by including horses that had no chance of placing. Of course, that long shot could come in, so he had to be very careful not to eliminate any dark horse.

He had become a whiz at compiling the statistics into a spreadsheet. He could sort by jockey, re-sort by the horse's speed in his last race, re-sort by those horses who won their last race, plus any other of twelve categories. The horses that came out consistently in the top half would automatically feed into a linked spreadsheet.

Pete started the download of the report from Santiago, who Pete believed to be the best handicapper in the business. He had won a considerable amount of money following Santiago's advice. After reading the numerous stories written about his exploits, Pete felt he almost knew Santiago personally.

Santiago had spent a good part of his life as a jockey, and he had been a good one. He listened to the body language of his mount. However, his luck ran out one day in an eight-furlong stakes race. His horse stumbled when another horse cut him off at the rail. The horse fell and Santiago's leg was caught underneath his mount as he went down. The fall severely damaged his left leg and ended his career as a jockey at age thirty-seven.

For several years, Santiago sank into the abyss of alcohol-induced depression and became a very bitter man. At forty-five, he suddenly sprang back on the scene, but this time as a handicapper. He capitalized on his ability to understand what was going on from the horse's demeanor. He became famous as he uncannily eliminated the bottom half of a field in a race. With the remaining field, the likely top contenders at least in his mind, he put together wagers called exotics.

The exotics allowed the everyday race fan to build a bet consisting of several horses in each finishing position. Santiago particularly liked the exotic known as the *exacta box*. He picked two, three, four, or more horses that he liked and *boxed* them. Any one combination of the boxed horses, placing first and second gave him a win. If the box happened to include a long shot coming in first or second with big odds, the win could be anywhere from hundreds to several thousands of dollars.

He also had a preference for an exotic known as the *trifecta*. A trifecta wager was similar to an exacta except he had to pick the first three finishers of a race in the correct order. Another type of exotic, the *superfecta*, he stayed away from. It was just too hard to pick the top four finishers.

Santiago's website and daily blog gave the subscriber background information on all the horses in a given race at a given meet. He didn't handicap all the races of a meet, only those where he felt he had an edge. Along with the backgrounds of the horses, jockeys, and owners, he put together statistics so the home-gamer could design his or her bets.

Online-betting websites were growing fast, both in number and popularity, especially when a race such as the Kentucky Derby was being hyped. Santiago was becoming a very rich man, not only from the subscribers to his website but also from his handicapping newsletter. In addition, he was cleaning up with his own exotic wagers.

Race day was special for Pete. He was still muttering because he didn't have a chance to download Santiago's updated report the night before, due to the auction and all the attention the press and the locals heaped on him.

Pete had been exhausted when he and Hutch returned to his condo, so after a beer he went straight to bed. His plan was to get up early to edit his spreadsheets with the very latest information and this he did.

He wasn't going to take the time for his morning shower which was always a chore. He had to maneuver his wheelchair just right into the shower stall, transfer his body to the shower chair and then shove the wheelchair away from the reach of the water. After bathing, he would repeat the process in reverse order. It was tricky because he could easily slip and fall if he wasn't careful.

Today he would skip the shower routine and get right to work on his handicapping. It was going to be a great day at Churchill Downs. He already had his winner, Big Brown, but he still had to pick his next six or seven wannabe-placers in order to design his exotic bets.

Pete particularly liked the exacta and the trifecta wagers. The problem today was many fans were going to pick Big Brown. Because this horse was a favorite, Pete could actually end up losing money, depending on which horses he picked to come in behind him. Or the possibility, horrible as it might be to imagine, that Big Brown wouldn't come in first.

Picking the second and third place horse was key. Here is where he could make some real dough. Then he dreamed of parlaying his winnings into the second leg of the Triple Crown, the Preakness, which would run in two weeks.

— • • • —

PETE'S DREAM of parlaying his winnings came closer to reality by the end of the day. Big Brown won the Kentucky Derby by four-and-a-half lengths!

Chapter 25

—•••—

DAYTONA BEACH INTERNATIONAL AIRPORT rarely displayed a lot of hustle and bustle, but this Saturday morning was especially serene. Catherine parked her car in the designated lot for travelers who were leaving for more than one day. She opened the car's trunk and grabbed the handle of her small suitcase. Before she could lift the case, a strong arm reached around and put his hand over hers. She turned her head to the left at the same time Hutch gave her a quick kiss on her neck.

"Good morning, Miss Catherine," Hutch said, giving her a big smile. "You must have slept more than a wink because you look fresh as a daisy." With the suitcase out of the trunk, he asked, "Do you have everything out of the car?"

A little flustered from the unexpected kiss on the neck, his cologne, his arm around her shoulders, she managed to say, "Do you always come up behind a lady and give her an unexpected kiss in the parking lot? Just let me grab my purse and sweater, and then I'm ready to be whisked away."

"Glad to hear you're ready, and, no, I don't go around kissing ladies in the parking lot unless she is a lovely lady named Catherine."

Hutch took Catherine's left hand, pulling her rolling suitcase with his other hand. He guided her to the front entrance of the airport, and then to a door that led to the tarmac and a plane waiting to take them to Washington. The flight was smooth, and in less than two hours, they landed at Andrew's Air Force Base. Hutch thanked the pilot for the ride and led Catherine to his car. He had parked at the base the day before when he headed south to be with Pete.

Washington was a blaze of spring blooms. The cherry blossoms had come and gone, but they were replaced with a palette of beautiful colors from pink roses to multi-color dahlias and blue delphiniums. Catherine had been to Washington several times but not in late spring.

She loved every minute of the ride from the base. It was especially enjoyable because Hutch held her hand as if she would somehow disappear.

"I made a reservation for you at the Franklin Inn," he said. "Thought we would stop so you can register, and then we'll go on to my house. I'll show you around and then give you some lunch. You must be starved."

"Whatever you say, my agent. I feel as if I'm in a dream—a very nice one."

He pulled into the drive of the Franklin Inn and asked the valet not to park the car, for they would be leaving shortly. Catherine signed in at the front desk and the porter led the way to her room along with her bag. The porter unlocked the room's door and deposited her bag on the luggage rack. Hutch tipped him and the attendant retreated, closing the door behind him. It was a beautiful room, cozy, and comfortable with elegant dark cherry colonial furniture.

"Do I need to take something else for dinner, or am I dressed okay?" she asked.

"You're perfect." Hutch took her in his arms. "But wait just one minute. I've wanted to kiss you again since the airport parking lot." He held her to him, slowly lowering his lips to hers. The warmth of the embrace rose between the two of them. Lifting his head and looking into her large brown eyes, he said, with a slightly husky voice, "Now, my dear, we can proceed with our day. I thought we would stay very casual and just hang out at my place. Maybe go down the street to a little Italian spot for dinner. I'm sure you'll be exhausted by then after the hoopla of the auction yesterday and traveling today."

"Sounds like a plan. I guess I'm ready to see that home of yours."

—•••—

IN THE CAR AGAIN, Hutch expertly maneuvered through the Saturday lunchtime traffic. He flipped out his cell phone and selected a number he had stored. "Hi, Rosie, it's Hutch. Can you make up one of those salmon salads of yours, a couple of rye rolls, and a medium fruit compote? Good. I'm about fifteen minutes away. ...thanks. Does the menu sound okay to you?" he said, turning to Catherine, giving her hand a quick kiss.

"Nice to see you in action, Agent Hutchinson. I'll not worry about you starving with a gal named Rosie on the other end of the line."

Hutch pulled up in front of a small neighborhood delicatessen. "I'll be right back. Don't let anybody kidnap you while I'm getting our lunch," Hutch said, as he leaned over and gave her another peck on the cheek. *This kissing is getting to be a habit,* he thought. *I haven't enjoyed myself like this for years, maybe ever.*

With their lunch in Catherine's lap, Hutch drove a few short blocks and pulled into his parking spot behind his house. "You understand, Catherine, parking anywhere in the District, is iffy at best. The fact I have my own parking, behind *my* house I might add, is a real luxury."

Helping her out of the car, Hutch grabbed the sacks holding their lunch. He led her to a gate in the middle of a high wooden fence. "Come with me, my dear, into the inner sanctum of my humble life."

The gate opened into a private courtyard. The birds were singing, and the scent of fresh-mown grass greeted the couple as they made their way along the cobblestone path to the back door. Hutch unlocked the door and, balancing the lunch bags and his briefcase, he pushed the door wide so Catherine could enter.

"What would you like, Catherine, a tour of the house or a bite to eat with a glass of wine?"

"I would like a glass of wine with a tour."

"Hey, wait till you see my wine cellar. A glass of Pouilly-Fuisse it will be. Just give me a minute."

Catherine walked around admiring the kitchen with gray granite counter tops. Then she went into the dining room where French doors opened onto a screened-in porch.

"Your wine, madam. Let's drink to a wonderful two days together." He tapped his glass to hers. Hutch put his glass down on the dining room table, gently took her shoulders, and pressed her to him as he bent to kiss her, a light but lingering kiss. Releasing her, he said, "Catherine, I'm so glad you agreed to come to Washington so I could show you my world."

"I'm delighted I came, too," Catherine said softly.

Hutch showed her around his house—three levels, all white walls. "You can see I need help. I haven't done anything since I bought the place except for a few pieces of necessary furniture. You know the basics, couch, beds, chairs, tables, some rugs."

"Don't be so hard on yourself. It looks comfortable, and I'm sure it works with your busy schedule, but, oh my goodness, the potential," Catherine said, turning to look at the room from different vantage points.

"Ah, that's what I wanted to hear. Let's eat our salads. We can talk out on the back porch. I think it's warm enough. How about a little more wine?"

"Love it. Let me help you. I guess we can use this tray. It's lovely. Where did you find it?"

"On one of the trips to Rio de Janeiro."

After lunch, Hutch put on a pot of coffee, which they took into the living room and the comfort of the over-stuffed couch and chair. Rachmaninoff's Concerto Number two played softly in the background.

—•••—

THE DAY SPED BY. Daylight melted into moonlight. Catherine and Hutch walked two blocks down the street from his house to a neighborhood Italian restaurant. It was obvious he dined there often, for the owners came out of the kitchen to greet him and to catch a glimpse of the beautiful lady on his arm.

After dinner, he drove her back to the inn. Escorting her to her room he again put his arms around her, but this time the kiss was gentle and sweet. Pulling away, he said, "Thank you for a most wonderful day. I know you must be tired, so I'll say goodnight. We have the whole day tomorrow to look forward to. Okay if I come by around eight-thirty in the morning? There's this delightful coffee shop down by the tidal basin. Then I thought a stroll around a few monuments and shops. There's a wonderful little café for lunch then back here to the inn to change for dinner. Is that too much?"

"It all sounds wonderful. I'll see you in the morning."

Hutch kissed her again. The kiss began to deepen, but he pulled away. "I'd better leave. Thank you again for today and tomorrow will be even better." With a smile he walked out closing the door behind him.

— • • • —

SUNDAY TURNED OUT to be everything Hutch had promised it would be. They walked. They talked. They shared stories from their pasts. He never let go of her. Her hand was always in his, or his arm was around her shoulders or her waist. Early afternoon they returned to the inn and a bottle of champagne in a silver ice bucket on the gleaming glass coffee table.

"I wonder if all their guests return in the afternoon to a bottle of champagne?" she asked.

"Only special guests," he said with a twinkle in his eye. "May I pour you a glass?"

"Yes. Please."

Hutch poured the champagne into two crystal flutes standing next to the silver ice bucket. He handed a flute to Catherine. "To a most beautiful woman. You made my day sparkle with your laughter and your presence beside me."

Hutch set his glass on the marble-top table, took her glass from her hand, and set it next to his. Taking her in his arms, they kissed in a heated embrace. The warmth of their bodies rose as one. He wanted this woman as he had never wanted a woman before. They sank down on the sofa, the embrace becoming more urgent. Hutch heard a ringing somewhere, but he couldn't register what it was. The ringing didn't stop. He realized it was his cell phone. He sat up still looking into Catherine's eyes. "I have to answer this. Forgive me." He could barely speak.

"Whoa! What did you say? That is a real break. Yes, yes, I'll get down there as soon as I can. I should be able to make it in a couple of hours."

Hutch broke the connection on his cell and started pacing. The mood in the room had changed with the phone call.

"That call. Did something bad happen?" Catherine asked.

"A break in a case." Hutch looked at her. "I'm sorry. I have to get to the airport right away. A plane is waiting for us. Can you get your things together? We'll check you out and head back to Andrews. I'll drop you off at the Daytona Beach Airport."

While Catherine put the few items she brought back in her suitcase, Hutch checked that the jet was fueled and on standby for his arrival. This time he would pilot the aircraft.

Flying back to Daytona, Hutch didn't say much to Catherine. He was agitated and frustrated. The day-and-a-half he spent with her gave him a glimpse of what his existence might be like if she were a part of his life.

Chapter 26

— • • • —

WHILE FLYING FULL THROTTLE from Andrews Air Force Base to Daytona Beach, Hutch's boss filled him in over the phone about the tip they had received.

"Hutch, as I told you earlier someone called regarding John Anderson," the Director said. "Our operator couldn't tell if it was a man or a woman. Let's say it was a man. The caller sounded old, but it could have been because of a raspy voice from smoking. The person said he knew John Anderson and that the Molly C was home ported near Caracas, Venezuela. The informant agreed to meet someone from the agency at Pablo's, a bar along the waterfront at Port of La Guaira. The informant said he would call back in four hours to set up the meeting. Then the line went dead."

"What logistics have you set up so far?" Hutch asked.

"The agency rented a small jet plane in Miami to fly you and the pilot to Caracas. The pilot is an agent to provide you with backup. We have a contact, a farmer with no allegiance to Chavez, within twenty minutes of the port. There's an old airstrip on his farm, almost overgrown with underbrush, but usable for a small plane. Both you and the pilot will travel undercover."

Hutch disconnected the call. He had to get to Miami, connect with his backup, and fly to Caracas as soon as possible. En route to Daytona Beach, all he could do was wait for the next communication with the exact time for the rendezvous with the informant. But more important, who was he meeting?

Catherine was sitting in the co-pilot seat next to him. Hutch reached for her hand, running his fingers softly over her skin. Turning her hand over he kissed her palm softly. "This will have to do until I can get back to you. I'm so sorry our weekend holiday came to such an abrupt end."

"It's okay, really. When duty calls, *duty calls*. Do you have any idea how long you'll be gone?"

"I never know. I'll call you if I get a chance, but you must know that I probably won't be able to communicate with you. That, my dear, will be the hardest part of this little trip."

Shit. Hutchinson thought. This sudden assignment is but a little taste of what it would be like if you entered into a relationship with this incredible woman. You have to be extra vigilant that you don't let your mind wander back to her. You've witnessed buddies killed for such lapses.

The plane touched down at the Daytona Beach Airport. It was on the ground only long enough to let Catherine disembark onto the tarmac with her bag. Hutch held her in his arms for a brief second, kissed her quickly, and then she walked away toward the terminal building. She turned and gave him a wave.

He waved back.

"See you soon," he said. He knew she couldn't hear his voice because of the noise of the jet, but he said it anyway. The stairs were pulled away, the door closed, and the plane, whose engines had never stopped, taxied down the runway, and took off over the trees flying due south to Miami.

Chapter 27

— • • • —

"HEY, JJ, FANCY SEEING YOU HERE," Hutch said, hugging his old buddy, giving him a slap on the back.

"You, too, my man. Long time since we worked together."

Jerry Johnstone, JJ for short, was recruited into the Homeland Security Agency the same time as Hutch. They had worked a few missions together and each respected the others intellect and bravery under extreme life-threatening circumstances. The two men were of the same height, build, and age, but JJ kept his head bald.

"When I saw your name as Operation Leader, I signed on immediately," JJ said. "Looked like old times south of the border in our fav city, Caracas. I'm not nuts about this antique plane they gave me to fly. It must have been the first jet ever built. Hell, I'm not sure it will even get off Miami's hallowed runway let alone get us to Port of La Guaira. Strap yourself in. You might as well ride shotgun," JJ said, laughing. "I figure our ETA around midnight. At least, I think this baby can make it in four hours."

Hutch fastened his seatbelt just as JJ gently pulled the plane's nose up into the blue skies over the Atlantic and just as his cell phone rang. An agent was calling from Washington. Hutch asked him to patch JJ in so they both could hear. The agent honored the request and then filled them in on the latest communication from the tipster.

"The meeting is set up for the morning siesta at eleven o'clock, still at Pablo's on the waterfront of the port. The tipster's instructions are to go into the bar, sit at a table, far left side, as far back as possible. Enter exactly at eleven, alone. Order Brahma beer with lime. The tipster will wait five to ten minutes and then walk over and ask if you have a cigarette. You are to say yes, and then ask the person to have a seat. The tipster will ask if you always drink Brahma beer. You are to answer 'only when I'm drinking at Pablo's.' If the tipster feels everything is okay to stay in the bar to talk, he will join you, if not, he will give you further directions. I still couldn't tell if it's a man or a woman, but I'm pretty sure from the gravelly voice that it's a man. He must be at least fifty."

"Okay, I got it," Hutch said. "JJ is waving a wad of bills at me. I guess I should be good to get a nice buzz on." Hutch held the phone away from his ear when the agent on the other end started swearing. "Hey, hey, only kidding. We're touchy today, aren't we? ...Yes, I know this isn't funny. Talk to you later," Hutch said cutting the connection.

The farmer had placed a few lights at the beginning and end of the dirt strip. There was also an electrical hookup to power the plane's computers without draining the batteries. JJ landed the plane as gently as a feather floating to earth. The two agents climbed out and walked over to a man standing next to some bushes. They shook hands, and the three men proceeded to douse the lights. The farmer disappeared into the vegetation. Hutch and JJ climbed back into the plane and settled down for the night.

The plane's seats were removed in the small cabin and replaced with cots anchored to the floor. Duffel bags contained several changes of clothes. The two men had everything they needed for a couple of days if the operation lasted that long.

In the morning, Hutch and JJ made their way to the docks on the bicycles JJ had stowed on the plane. A cruise ship loomed at one of the piers along with several freighters. Behind the piers was a hill, almost a mountain, dotted with small huts or shanties. The huts were so close together that some appeared to be joined. Hutch had been told that most of the dwellings had electricity but no running water. As primitive as life seemed to be on this hillside, almost all of the huts had a satellite dish attached to the outside of the structure.

Pablo's wasn't hard to find. It seemed every guy around the docks knew of it. However, the bar didn't get any glowing reports. Hutch asked about the bar in Spanish and quickly took on the dialect of the dock workers. As the two buddies had planned, JJ had Hutch's back, trailing far enough behind so no one would notice but close enough so he wouldn't lose him in the crush of the tourists queuing up to board the ship. It was 9:53 a.m. when Hutch spotted Pablo's ahead. The cruise ship blasted its horn to signal that it was ready to depart.

Several laggard groups of passengers quickly headed for her and the next leg of their journey.

At precisely eleven o'clock Hutch, in a well-worn, white T-shirt and jeans, sauntered into the bar. There were only a few patrons. Hutch surmised they were mostly dock workers from their clothing and general grimy appearance. He looked around. If someone was watching, he would look to be deciding where to sit. He walked to his left and found a table towards the back as the informant had instructed. No one sat nearby. He pulled a chair away from under the table and swung it around. He sat down, straddling the chair with his back against the wall. He could see the front door and also most of the bar, now to his left.

The bar was hot and humid. Obviously, Pablo didn't believe in air conditioning, or he couldn't afford it, or he didn't care. His customers were used to the heat. Four or five ceiling fans lazily churned the air. The red tile floor was scratched but clean, as were the black Formica tabletops. The rattan chairs, no cushions, were worn but sturdy.

The bartender came over for his order. "Pablo" was embroidered on his shirt. At least Hutch thought it was Pablo, a little hard to tell because most of the stitching was gone. Hutch ordered a local brew, a Brahma.

"You're a stranger here, señor," Pablo said. "I haven't seen you before."

"I'm just passing through unless I find a job," Hutch replied in Spanish and shrugged his shoulders. He pulled out a cigarette and lit it. "If I find a job, then who knows how long I'll stay. I could become a regular."

Pablo went to fetch the beer. On his way back to the table another customer came in, JJ. He sat at the counter. When Pablo returned to the bar and asked the man what he would like, JJ spoke in English.

Five minutes later a woman approached Hutch. "Hola, can you spare a cigarette, por favor?" She wasn't old, but she wasn't young either. He thought the agency had guessed her age about right, but not the sex. She was neat as a pin with a white short-sleeved shirt tucked into blue jeans, strapped tight with a tan leather belt studded with turquoise stones. Her black shiny hair, tucked behind her ears, had a few streaks of gray peeking out of her turquoise billed cap. Her voice was indeed raspy, obviously from a lifetime addiction to tobacco. Her body was trim and straight. Her hand when she reached for the cigarette appeared to be weathered and calloused from hard work.

"You new here, eh, señor?" the woman said in English.

"Hey, Coco," Pablo called out. "I bet if you asked nicely, the stranger will buy you a beer to go with that cigarette," he said with a chuckle from the end of the counter.

"How bout it, señor? I never try a beer like you have."

"Si, Pablo, por favor." Hutch raised his bottle and pointed to the woman.

Pablo hustled over with the beer. "See, Coco, I tell you better days are coming."

Coco sat down facing Hutch, her back to the door and the bar. No one could see if she was talking. She leaned back in her chair and put her feet up on the seat next to her. In a soft voice, she asked, "Señor, do you always drink Brahma beer?"

"Only when I'm drinking at Pablo's." Hutch thought Coco seemed to be satisfied with his answer, so he waited to see what she would say next.

"Señor, you know my name. What is yours?" she asked, flicking ashes into the tin ashtray.

"Hutch. You can call me Hutch. So, Señora Coco, to what do I owe the pleasure of your company?"

"Well, señor, first let me ask what brought you here?"

"A phone call. Did you call me?"

"Si, señor. I saw on the television the story about Señor John Anderson and his boat Molly C. The story say they not know where the boat come from. I know this, but I don't think I remember everything so good, if you know what I mean, señor?"

"Si, señora, I know what you mean. How much do you think it would take to help you remember...to help you remember everything?"

"Señor Hutch, you seem like a nice man, but I know you have much money you can access."

"Señora Coco, let us not play games. You will be rewarded depending on what you know. So far all you say is you know *this*. Señora, what is *this*? Give me something to believe you, por favor."

"Fair enough, Señor Hutch. I have been Señor Anderson's housekeeper for the past two years. He lives, or rather lived, not far from here. He had his own dock where he kept his boat."

"I see, señora, but this story has been on the television for almost two weeks. Why didn't someone else call with this information? Why you, señora?"

"Good point, señor. I tell you why. John Anderson was known here as John Jackson. It wasn't until just before he left, that he changed the name of his boat. The new name was painted by my friend Pedro. He also worked for John as a gardener. At least he says he is a gardener, but I'm not so sure. You see, when I work at the big house, I keep my mouth shut and my ears open."

"Where can I find this Pedro?" Hutch asked.

"I'm not sure, señor. My memory is getting a bit foggy."

"I see. Before your memory is completed fogged up, let me ask you, do you know where this John Anderson came from?"

"Si, señor. He said he came from Michigan in your United States. He said his mother and father died leaving him a lot of money. He always became very irritated when he spoke of his parents. They were very strict with him as a boy, making him work for every penny he earned. He hated them and was happy when they were gone. He also hated your United States. He would often say he would show those *imperialists*, whatever that means."

"Señora, if you can give me a piece or two more information about Señor Anderson, so I can check him out, to verify your story, I think we may come to an agreement. For instance, did he ever indicate he was in the military service, and from what city in Michigan did he come from?"

"That is easy, señor. He was in the Army. Oooh, I shudder to think how much he would rant and rave how he hated the Army and was glad when his service ended three years ago. He said he lived in Lansing, Michigan."

"Señora Coco, I will leave now to check this information. It will take me a few hours. Could we meet for dinner?"

"Si, señor. There is a fish vendor down by the last pier. There are outdoor tables and benches. It is really for the touristas so not many locals go down that far. I will meet you there at eight o'clock tonight."

"I'll see you then, señora." Hutch stood up to leave. He turned his chair back around and slid it under the table. "Can I give you another cigarette before I go?"

"Si, señor. That would be nice, gracias."

Hutch left the bar and sauntered back down the street. He and JJ had chained their bicycles about three-quarters of a mile away from the piers. He started to walk faster as he left the little tourist shops behind and retrieved his bike. It wasn't long before JJ caught up with him, and they rode down the dirt lane to the farm.

Hutch called the agency and gave them as much as he had on John Anderson, otherwise known as John Jackson, Lansing, Michigan, Army, wealthy parents, left the service three years ago.

"I have to verify there is such a person, his Army record, and any information on his current whereabouts," Hutch requested. "I have to have it by this afternoon. Also, email me his picture if you can get it from his Army ID."

"Whew, that's a pretty tall order for a few hours," JJ said after Hutch finished his conversation. "I heard the bartender call your friend Coco. I take it she had some info?"

"Yes, but you heard all I have so far—not much except for a couple of interesting tidbits. She said a gardener called Pedro painted the name Molly C on the boat not long before Anderson headed for Miami. Coco was his housekeeper. She wouldn't give me anything more until I gave her something for her foggy memory."

Hutch opened the little refrigerator and pulled out two bottles of iced tea.

"If we can verify this is the same guy, I think she has a lot more she can tell us. I have a date to meet her tonight at eight o'clock at the end of the last pier. How much did your office give you for an informant payoff?"

"A hundred Gs."

"Good. That should be more than enough to lift the fog from Señora Coco's memory."

Chapter 28

—•••—

ANOTHER BEAUTIFUL DAY IN PARADISE, Catherine thought with a heavy sigh, as she drove through the lunch-hour traffic on Ridgewood Avenue to International Speedway. She still felt a letdown because of the abrupt end to her weekend with Hutch. She turned right onto Beach Street and a couple of blocks later pulled into the parking lot of Pelican Bay Marina.

SUVs hauling boat trailers parked in one section near the boat ramp. A Jaguar, Corvette, and BMW sat in reserved spots. The owners were either out on their boats or grabbing a bite to eat in the lounge. Staff cars parked around back.

Catherine parked in one of the visitor spots and headed into the marina. Ted Adams greeted her at the door.

"Catherine, it is so good to see you," he said, shaking her hand.

"You have quite an operation going here, Ted."

Inside, the marina buzzed with activity. The cashier at the bar checked out one group of patrons returning to work after lunch just as another group headed out to their boats for an afternoon of sun, fun, and fishing.

"It's a little crazy at times especially as lunch winds down, but I'm glad you saw the hubbub before they all left. Another group will wander in about two this afternoon, mostly retired, to have a drink with friends. Come with me, I want to show you the space I'm considering for the new dining room."

Ted led Catherine along the bar and then outside through a wall of sliding glass doors. The chatter became muted as they walked along a small deck with five blue and white-striped umbrella tables. Along the far edge, a railing separated the deck from an overgrown piece of land that looked like a conservation area—oak trees with Spanish moss hanging off branches, palmetto plants, and a thick undergrowth of various bushes. Catherine had no idea what some of the specimens were.

"This is the beginning of the space I'd like to expand and incorporate into an indoor and outdoor dining area," Ted explained. "The lounge we just walked through could also be part of the space. I would extend the existing building into this overgrown area, plus enlarge the patio dining. I envision the main entrance to the new dining area to be where the lounge is now. Patrons could park, come in the front entrance of the marina, and go straight to the dining room. I would also have to accommodate the boaters who just want to grab a quick bite, a snack bar of some sort."

"What are you going to do about additional parking?" Catherine asked.

"The property extends three acres to the south and north about the same," Ted replied. "You're right, parking has to be addressed. I have plenty of boat storage so that's not an issue. With the expansion, I'll also increase the number of slips and docks for mooring along the river in front of the dining room. The improvements will provide guests with a wonderful view as boats dock or take off down the river. And, of course, there's the beauty of the river itself. We could even add a second floor, which would give a spectacular panorama above all the boats looking out over the water."

"You've obviously done your research as to the viability of such a project," Catherine said. "Without any plans to go by, my guess is you will be able to accommodate an additional seventy to eighty people at a seating, especially if you add a second floor."

"You know, that's the number I had in mind," Ted said. "I don't want it so big it loses its charm, but eighty more seats should work well. A second floor dining room could also be rented out for functions. Of course, this means expanding the kitchen to handle additional food prep."

"Ted, do you have a blueprint for the present building and a plot plan of your land?" Catherine asked, as she began to see the potential beauty of the view that would give an exclusive dining experience to the patrons. "I'm sorry. I may be getting ahead of myself. You haven't offered me the job. However, I would like the plans so I could run some ideas past Russell Stone to see if he's interested in the firm taking on the project, and if he wants me to head the design team."

"I know I want to proceed with Stone and Associates, and from what he's told me about you, I'm sure you're perfect for the project. Let's go to my office. I put a set of blueprints in a tube for you."

Ted's office was a comfortable room. It housed a large desk with a couple of chairs facing it. The bay window on the left looked out on the boat storage building. Inside the bay window was a comfortable seating area with two small overstuffed chairs in light blue microfiber, and two love seats facing each other across a glass coffee table. The glass floated on top of a concrete statue of a dolphin. The dolphin's tail was spread wide so the glass had three points of support—the snout and two tail fins.

Just as Ted handed the blueprints to Catherine, a man in a bathing suit came running through the door calling Ted's name.

"Ted we have a problem on mooring three. A member is complaining that there's a spike from the piling about a foot under water. It scraped the hull of his boat. He's sure the spike is going to rupture the boat's skin. He's demanding to see you."

"Okay, I'm on my way. Let me put on swim trunks so I can get in the water. Catherine, you have to excuse me. Here are the blueprints. Call me when you have some ideas, and we'll set up a meeting."

"I will, Ted, and good luck with the mooring." Catherine took the rolled up plans and headed for the front door. As she approached the entrance, she could see through the lounge window at what must have been the mooring in question. Two men in swimsuits were talking with an obviously upset man in his mid sixties sporting a protruding beer belly. Ted walked quickly past Catherine, said goodbye, and slipped out the side door. He wore a pair of swim trunks and a pale blue T-shirt with a white pelican on the front. As he exited the lounge door, he pulled off his shirt and sprinted down to the dock.

Catherine was impressed with Ted's physique, washboard abs, strong shoulders and biceps. A bit curious, she went over to the lounge window to watch the action.

Chapter 29

—•••—

FOR THE SECOND TIME in one day, Hutch made his way to the last pier at Port of La Guaira. JJ followed far behind him but within eyesight.

As Hutch approached the tables Coco described a few hours earlier, he saw her. She sat with her feet up on the bench, her hat pulled down, sucking on a dark brown bottle. As he came nearer she looked up. They exchanged greetings, both keeping their hands to themselves. No wave. No handshake. Just two people happening to share the same space.

"Your information turned out to be accurate, Coco," Hutch said, sitting on the other side of the bench. "I guess we can do some business. I want to get into Anderson's house, look around? You'll let me in?"

"Si, señor, for a price," Coco said, peeking out from under the bill of her cap.

"And what would that price be?"

"Thirty-thousand dollars—ten for the phone call, ten for the information I gave you, and ten for getting you into his house. One more thing, you must give me the money now. Do you understand, señor?"

"Si, señora, I understand. I have forty-thousand in my pocket. I will give you the money as you request, plus another ten when I leave you, just in case that foggy memory of yours clears with additional information. Is this agreeable to you?"

"Si, this is agreeable."

Hutch pulled out four ten-thousand-dollar bundles. He handed over three of the bundles and placed them in Coco's outstretched palm. He stuffed the remaining one back into his pocket. Of course, Hutch had many pockets in his cargo pants.

"Come, señor, we walk to the house. Only take us twenty minutes if we hurry." Darkness was descending, providing some cover as they walked, plus it was a rare cloudy night.

They strode down a road full of potholes. It was bordered on the land side by a creek. The bullfrogs croaking up a storm, and the crickets communicating, were the only sounds, muting their footfalls cushioned by rubber soles.

"Señora Coco, this morning you mentioned a gardener, a Pedro, I believe. Will he be at the house tonight?"

"Oh no, señor. I've only seen him once since Señor Anderson left his dock for Miami. Pedro came by the day after the news was on the television that Señor Anderson was dead. He came to the house to collect his money. He said Señor Anderson told him he could come and get it anytime if he didn't hear from him when he reached Miami."

"Did he get his money?" Hutch asked.

"I suppose so. He went to Señor Anderson's office in the house. I didn't pay much attention, but I did see him leave awhile later. I was a little surprised because he had a box full of something he lugged out to his car. I suppose it was some plans for the garden. They were always talking about planting this or that. I pay no attention to them."

Hutch and Coco soon arrived at the house. Hutch was surprised at how unpretentious it looked from the outside. The home was no bigger than a medium-sized ranch house, similar to so many track houses he had seen dotting the neighborhoods of Los Angeles. It was made of stucco, topped with red tiles. Anderson's dock was also not very long. Knowing the length of the Molly C, Hutch surmised there couldn't have been more than a few yards of clearance on either end, let alone dredged deep enough to keep her afloat.

He followed Coco around to the back door where she pulled out a key letting them in.

"Coco, let's not turn on the lights. I have a flashlight so I can take a quick look around. Let's keep this visit to ourselves."

"Si, señor. I want no one to know I let you in. I certainly don't want anyone to know of my call to you. I live in a room off the kitchen. I will go in and turn on the lights, like I normally do."

"Before you go to your room, can you show me the office?"

"Si, señor. Follow me." Coco led him down a hall to the living room which faced the water and the dock. "This is the room he called his office. We passed his bedroom on the left."

"Thanks, Coco. I'll stop to see you before I leave."

The air in the house was musty. Coco obviously hadn't opened any windows since the owner had left. It didn't take Hutch long to discover the hard drive from Anderson's computer was missing. The desk drawers were emptied of all paper. *It seems Pedro did a thorough job*, Hutch thought. The only thing he spotted was a maritime map of the Atlantic showing Caracas on the bottom and Miami just above it. He put it in one of his pockets. After searching the room, he retraced his steps back to what Coco said was Anderson's bedroom. Nothing seemed disturbed or out of the ordinary.

Hutch went back to the kitchen and called to Coco. She came out of her room and closed the door behind her, so they were in the dark. "Coco, tell me what you know about Pedro. From your description of when he left the house with a box of stuff, as you said, I think he took more than a paycheck."

"I am afraid of Pedro, señor. I don't want to talk about him. I know he would be very unhappy if he knew I called you, and especially if he knew I let you poke around this house."

"Why are you afraid of him?"

"He have a bad temper. I would often hear Pedro and the señor arguing. When an argument was particularly loud, I went into my room and turned the radio on high, or if it was really bad, I walk down to Pablo's."

"How old is Pedro? Where's he from? What's his last name? Come on, Coco, I gave you a lot of money. Give me some answers."

"Señor, I don't know the answer to these questions. I think he's from this area because he talks like us, but he also speaks English. He must be at least forty, I guess. I only know him by the name Pedro. Oh, wait a minute. There is a picture of Pedro and the señor down on the docks when they pulled in a big fish. It's in Señor Anderson's office."

Aided by his flashlight, Coco led Hutch back down the hallway to the office. She went over to a window. Hanging on the wall between the window and a bookcase were a framed graduation certificate from the University of Michigan and two pictures. One picture was of two men holding a fish and the other of a man Hutch did not recognize. The certificate stated Jackson received a Bachelor of Science degree in biochemistry. Coco took the picture of the men with a fish from the wall and handed it to Hutch.

"Coco, I'm taking both of the pictures and the framed certificate with me. Thanks, you've been a big help. Here's the other ten-thousand dollars I said may come your way. We'll call it your foggy-memory fund. If anybody asks you about me, tell them I was a stranger passing through who gave you a couple of cigarettes at Pablo's. You know how to reach me. Just call the number you called before. Ask to speak to Hutch. I'll be on the line before you know it."

"Si, señor, Hutch," she said, her lips turned up slightly in a smile. "I don't know what happened to Señor Anderson, but being shot, it can't be good. God be with you, señor."

Chapter 30

— ••• —

SNAPPING HIS PROSTHETIC LEGS in place, Daytona Pete stepped to the bedroom closet pulling out a pair of long chino pants and a black golf shirt. A pair of barely-worn sneakers were already on the feet of his legs. Looking in the mirror, he saw a middle-aged guy, but others would see a rather rugged man with black hair, dark eyes, and a perpetual tan, in other words, an arresting figure.

Pete was dressing for his meeting with Catherine and Tillie at the House of Beads. Deep down he was excited about the prospect of lending his considerable knowledge to their cyber café plans. Outwardly, he was as calm as a sleeping cat on a pillow although a little irritated to be leaving his preparations for the Preakness.

"Let's see, where did I put that cologne?" Pete scratched around the top drawer of his bureau. "Ah, here you are," he said, slapping a little on his freshly-shaved cheeks and chin. "Okay, ladies, your consultant is ready," he said, talking to himself as usual. "At least I'll have someone else to chat with, but then I may get an answer I don't like," he said, chuckling.

Catherine had offered to pick him up, but he had declined. He hadn't given his car a run in the last few weeks, so it was time to put on his legs and get off his keister. He hadn't been using his legs regularly and he knew that after a couple of hours they would become uncomfortable, start chafing where they connected.

— ••• —

TILLIE PUT ON a fresh pot of coffee. Not just any coffee. She purchased the Hawaiian Kona Breakfast Blend for this special meeting. Carolyn, her assistant, was at the register processing a customer's credit card. Tillie didn't want any distractions when she met with Catherine and Daytona Pete.

Catherine was the first to arrive, and the two ladies immediately went next door to the vacant shop. Tillie had set up three chairs and a five-foot folding table for their papers. Tillie heard the little silver bell jingle in her shop but didn't pay any attention because Carolyn would take care of whoever it was.

"Tillie, I sent an email to Pete with some notes so we wouldn't completely blindside him," Catherine said, laying some schematics and color charts on the table. "I think—"

"Hello, ladies," Pete said, as he entered the shop. Catherine was stunned at the transformation from wheelchair bound to tall muscular man. Of course, he always had the muscles, but she just hadn't noticed them when they first met at the auction. If Catherine was stunned, Tillie was star struck.

Catherine recovered from her shock and quickly went to Pete. "Pete, you look terrific," she said shaking his hand. "I'd like you to meet the owner of the House of Beads, the shop next door, Tillie Brown."

"Glad to meet you, Daytona …Mr. Peterson."

"Please, call me, Pete," he said, taking Tillie's hand she offered.

"Here's your coffee, Tillie," Carolyn said. "I thought your guests might like more than one cup, so here's a carafe, nice and hot." She placed the coffee service at one end of the table and added some cookies Tillie had baked but forgot to tell her about. "That's some sporty red Thunderbird you have there," Carolyn said, looking out the window and then back to Pete.

"Thank you, young lady," Pete said smiling. "It does get me where I'm going with a little fun thrown in. Now this is what I call a proper meeting," Pete said, helping himself to a cookie. "Catherine, Tillie, may I pour you a cup of coffee?" Pete asked, thoroughly enjoying the obviously good impression he had made on the women.

Tillie didn't know what to say, other than, "Yes, please." Catherine accepted a cup as well, adding her thimble of cream. "Pete, now that you see the space, do you think the suggestions I emailed you will work?"

Pete set his cup down and walked with care to the door in the back of the shop. Catherine noted a slight swung to his gate but marveled at how well he moved. "As far as all the decorating stuff, I leave that to you ladies. Tillie, do you have a key to this door? I presume it is the back-office area. I'd like to see how much room we have for the computer set up."

"Yes, it's on this ring," she said, fumbling. "Here, you can find it quicker than I can." Tillie seemed to become more and more undone as the three discussed the plans.

Pete took the keyring from Tillie and quickly unlocked the door. "Well, this is bigger than I thought it would be. And, how nice the previous tenant left it clean as a whistle and some shelving to boot. There's plenty of room. You could dedicate a nice chunk to the computer and all the paraphernalia that comes with it. This wall on the shop side isn't concrete block, which will make it easier for direct wiring of ports to the Internet for customers who need security and prefer not to use a public hot spot. However, if I read the write-up correctly that you sent me, Catherine, on the company providing a turnkey operation, the setup is mostly wireless—great new technology."

Pete walked around the back office area, calculating the square footage in his head. He knocked on walls to determine their construction. He checked the keyring again to open the door leading to the shop's exterior entrance. The entrance was level with the interior as well as exterior walkway, something he always took note of in case he used his wheelchair. He closed the rear-entrance door and locked it. Returning to the shop area, he also locked the back office door and gave the keys back to Tillie. He topped off his coffee and sat down.

"I presume you're going to sell computer time on prepaid cards like the vendor suggests," Pete said. "One suggestion I have is to stock some brand of memory stick with a USB connection. If customers need to store a document, or retrieve information from the Internet, but didn't bring a portable flash drive, they could buy one from you. Don't look at it as a revenue stream, more as an amenity."

Catherine made a note of Pete's suggestion. "Thanks, Pete. By any chance would you be interested in setting up the equipment if we decide to go ahead?"

"I think I could take care of that little task. I can certainly cable the computers, install software, and test their operation. Mind you, I couldn't get involved until after the Belmont Stakes in New York. I have some stallions that require my undivided attention."

"Oh, I've heard all about your OTBP," Tillie said, finally coming out of her trance…somewhat. "We certainly wouldn't want to disturb you or interfere with your racing."

"Do you have any idea what you might charge as a consulting fee?" Catherine asked. "I'm trying to put together a business plan, and I need to determine the start-up costs."

"Well, let's see," Pete said, looking very stern, his brow furrowed. "Let's just say I might do it on a barter basis. You know, a bracelet here, a dinner there."

Chapter 31

— • • • —

IT WAS FIVE-THIRTY in the morning and eight days to the Preakness. Pete's eyes were wide open. He was so excited about starting his handicapping regimen that he couldn't sleep. The gurgling coffeepot beckoned him to get his lazy bones out of bed. He sat up grabbing his clothes off the wheelchair. At night when he prepared to go to bed, he laid his fresh clothes on the chair, positioning it next to the bed. In the morning, his clothes were within arm's reach and ready to go—into the shower, get dressed, coffee on his balcony.

He could hardly contain himself as his excitement grew. No matter how eager he was to start the day, he rarely altered his morning routine. Following the scent of the fresh-brewed coffee, he wheeled into the kitchen. A splash of cream went into the bottom of his man-sized cup, then the coffee. Flipping up the side tray tucked under the arm of his wheelchair, he carefully rolled to the sliding glass doors leading to the balcony. He pulled back the door and rolled out onto his balcony. It was too early for the sun; the inky darkness was punctuated with the crashing waves of the ocean—music to Pete's ears.

"What a beautiful way to begin the day," he said out loud. It was a good thing he lived alone because if a horse he bet on came in last, Pete swore up and down. "How could the stupid animal come in last? It should be shipped immediately to the glue factory." He wondered if his neighbors could hear his loud outbursts. But gosh darn it, the nag should have at least come in second.

This morning was especially sweet because he was going to start designing his wagers for the Preakness, the second leg of a potential triple crown in Belmont, New York. He also hoped to parlay his big winnings from the Derby into an even bigger bankroll. Santiago's blog would be posted this day, giving his first rationale for his Preakness picks and how he envisioned the race would be run. But for now, Pete was content to sit back in his chair, sipping the hot creamy liquid, dreaming of a big score. A few thoughts surfaced about his meeting with Catherine and Tillie, but he quickly pushed them aside. He had work to do.

A little before six o'clock, the horizon began to lighten. The sun inched its way up, letting everyone know on the east coast that a new day was dawning. Pete stayed on the balcony as the colors switched from a pale gray to light blue, to orange and gold, depending on the clouds around to catch the beams. Once the tip of the yellow ball breached the horizon, he turned his chair and went inside. No matter how good his sunglasses were, the sun's rays hurt his eyes. Anyway, it was time to get busy.

Three hours flew by as Pete switched from one handicapper to the other on the Internet. The post positions wouldn't be assigned until late the Wednesday before the race, so the information was all about the horses in general. How they were feeling, and when they were scheduled to arrive in Maryland. What jockeys had been picked, and which jockeys wouldn't get the thrill of riding in the Preakness. The hype on Big Brown, the Derby winner, was the lead item on all the handicappers' articles.

A little after ten o'clock, Pete checked again to see if Santiago's blog was posted with his scoop on the race. "Hallelujah, mama come to papa," Pete said as he hit the print command. While the blog printed, Pete fixed himself another cup of coffee. He wanted to enjoy reading Santiago's picks. He broke out a sugar-frosted chocolate doughnut left, per his request, by his part-time housekeeper.

"Thank goodness for Agnes," he said to himself. Agnes came four times a week, picking up the groceries from the list he emailed her the night before, plus anything else he might need. She'd drop off the groceries, run the dishwasher, and performed what other chores he had lined up for her. She spent two to four hours with him, depending on the length of the list and how much hollering she could stand if there happened to be a morning race somewhere in the world.

Pete settled back with his coffee and doughnut and began reading the blog. "Sure, Santiago, Big Brown will come in first. Now there's a hard call. How brilliant you are. Hell, even I know that much." He continued to read. When he reached the second to last paragraph he sat up sharply. His doughnut was long gone, but a splash of coffee hit the page and the front of his white T-shirt.

"Damn it. Santiago, you've got to be kidding. Gayego *last*? What the heck is this garbage? It doesn't make sense." Pete read the paragraph regarding the horse Gayego again. He was going to include Gayego in his wagering, various combinations from second, to third, and fourth place. He was even going to put together a superfecta— picking the first through fourth place finishers.

I don't get this gibberish, he thought to himself. He read the paragraph out loud. "I will have information tomorrow if Gayego should be warehoused. But will defer to Pedro if he spills the beans. Otherwise, my blog will blackout so this will not drone on and on without testing. Trainer is resting in Daytona Beach."

He threw the printout on the couch and wheeled to the sliding glass doors.

"What a bunch of horse shit," he said. "I pay this guy all kinds of money, and he gives me this beautiful animal should be warehoused? I don't believe it." He picked up the page again, reading through squinted eyes, to make sure he wasn't dreaming. "Wait a minute, maybe there's something else going on here."

Pete grabbed the wheel of his chair, jerking it forward so violently that he almost fell out. He attacked his computer's keyboard and typed out the paragraph about Gayego in his word processing program.

"Oh, my God, can this be what I think it is?" he said. He grabbed the telephone, punched in a number, and then hit the speaker button so he could talk, leaving his hands free for his keyboard. He heard the phone pick up and immediately barked at the instrument. "Hutch, you there? I've got to talk to you, now."

"Geez, Pete, what the hell's so urgent you can't let me say hello?"

"I'm working on my Preakness handicapping, and—"

"You called me, yelling like a banshee, because of a horse race?"

"Shut up, you bastard, and listen to me. No wait. I'm going to email you this paragraph while I read it to you." Pete quickly opened his email account, copied and pasted the paragraph into the message, and then clicked the send button. Not waiting for Hutch to open the email, he read the message to him.

"Pete, that's garbage. You've got to get yourself another hobby," Hutch said, as he accessed his email account from the plane's computer. "Okay, I got your message and that crazy information on Gayego."

"Okay, now underline every fifth word and read it back to me ...the underlined words."

"You really have become a nut case, you know that don't you? All right, here's what I come up with—tomorrow warehoused pedro beans blackout drone testing beach. So?"

"So? Don't you get it? Keep Daytona in there and read it again, you knucklehead. Out loud, if you please."

"Okay, okay, here goes. Tomorrow warehoused Pedro beans Daytona Beach blackout drone testing. Are you trying to tell me this is some kind of code about the ricin?"

"Yes, stupid, I am. I've been checking for Santiago's blog all morning and finally it was up. Let's see, I printed it at nine minutes after ten from the time stamp on the bottom of my sheet." As Pete talked, he logged into Santiago's website. Scrolling to the Gayego paragraph, he exclaimed, "Wait. Wait. Hutch, it's gone! I mean the paragraph I sent you has been replaced with why he thinks Gayego will be last, his timings, his finishes. My God, Hutch, it's gone."

"Hey, I think you're onto something. Maybe your Army training in cryptology finally paid off. I'm busy right now so I'll have to get back to you."

"What do you mean you're *busy?* Where the hell are you?"

"None of your business, nosy. Seeing how you're playing with the horses, take a few minutes and get me all the information you can on Santiago. Get me his full name and where you think he lives. You know, does he live in the States? Get whatever he gives as his background on the website. Email me as much as you can. I'll look for your information and then ship it to my office so they can dig deeper. Heck, just get me the basics in the next ten minutes so I can email the agency immediately. Depending what they come up with, and if I can wrap things up here, I will be at your place tomorrow morning."

Twenty minutes crept by before Hutch's screen lit up with the message, "You have mail." Pete's message was cryptic and to the point.

"Luis Santiago, born 1960 in Caracas, Venezuela. Professional jockey until hurt leg which ended his career at age 37. Became an alcoholic. Two years ago back on the scene as a handicapper, now age 46.

Love and kisses, Pete."

—•••—

PETE'S SCREEN echoed back that he had mail.

"Message received. Sending same to office. Brew that coffee for seven tomorrow morning.

Love and kisses, back at ya, Hutch."

—•••—

THREE PAIRS of eyes at three different locations, read Santiago's blog. Their instructions were clear—pack your bags and rendezvous tomorrow afternoon at the warehouse.

Chapter 32

—•••—

JJ FLEW HUTCH TO MIAMI and then returned to Caracas to find Pedro. Hutch hopped on a small government jet in Miami heading north to Daytona Beach. He called Manny from the air and set up a rendezvous at Pete's condo for 7:30 in the morning. He filled him in on the possible mysterious code Pete had intercepted in the handicapper's blog.

Hutch's head was spinning with all the information he had gleaned over the past forty-eight hours. He wanted to engage Manny and Pete into an operation that was forming in his head. On the way to Pete's place, he stopped, as instructed under penalty of no cooperation from Pete, to pick up a dozen assorted doughnuts, heavy on the glazed-chocolate variety.

When he pulled into the condo's visitor lot, he was pleased to see Manny's parked car. Hutch let himself into Pete's condo unit, nodded to each man, and set the doughnuts on the counter. Pete was wrapping up his suspicions to Manny about Santiago's blog.

Hutch and Manny slid on to the kitchen chairs as Pete indicated he'd roll over to the table with the coffeepot. Peaches sat in front of the sliding doors, whining whenever a pelican glided close by on the morning breeze.

"Let's start with what we know," Hutch said.

"What are the chances these guys are part of a cell of a bigger group, like Al-Qaeda?" Pete asked.

"In the agency's preliminary searches, there doesn't seem to be a nexus with any known terrorist group," Hutch replied. "The home grown fanatics and their disgruntled friends from other countries tend to stay under our radar, which of course makes them so dangerous. For instance, if the storm hadn't beached the Molly C, we would never have known of this little band of shitheads. Never have known, that is, until a bunch of people died. That's the bad news. The good news is that they have a tendency to make some kind of blunder that grabs our attention. Right now we have one body, John Anderson. Here, Manny, this is a picture I took from the wall in his house. He's definitely your John Doe. The man standing next to him is Pedro."

"No shit," Pete chimed in. "Do you think he's *the* Pedro in Santiago's blog?"

"I don't know yet, but my contact, Coco at Port of La Guaira, is going to find out all she can about him," Hutch said. "He was Anderson's gardener, but I suspect he did more than plant petunias. After the news of Anderson's death, he came by the house and told Coco he was going into the office to get his paycheck. Anderson was supposed to leave it for him. She saw Pedro leave with a big box of stuff. When I searched the office, which is really his living room, all papers were gone along with his computer's hard drive. Who knows what else was missing. Pete, can I use this easel pad? I promise I won't destroy your hen scratches."

"Yes, you can use it, and you'd better not destroy my hen scratches. They could be the beginning of a million bucks at Santa Anita tomorrow, eighth race."

"Ya, ya, and you can treat Manny and me to a dinner at the Ritz in Boston if that happens," Hutch retorted, flipping the scratched-up sheet to the back of the easel. "To move our theories along, let's stipulate that we have three men who seem to be involved, one way or another, in some kind of dirty deed—Santiago, Pedro, Anderson. Let's also stipulate the reference to beans in the blog means ricin from castor beans, and that the reference to pedro is *the* Pedro in Venezuela. The code appeared in Santiago's blog yesterday between ten and ten-thirty in the morning. The words were deleted or rather replaced about ten-thirty. So the reference to *tomorrow* means today. I would guess that they are to meet at a warehouse today. Pedro is supposed to bring the ricin, and further, they planned to test a drone as a delivery method."

"Okay, but where is this test supposed to take place? Daytona Beach?" Manny asked.

"Nah. They *have* to test in Baltimore, Pimlico Race Track, the Preakness Stakes, to be ready for Belmont," Pete said, staring at the easel pad. "And, if Santiago is calling the shots, it was his blog after all that alerted them to a meeting, the drone test will be in Baltimore. Hell, if Big Brown wins the freaking Preakness Saturday, the whole world is going to be watching a race for the Triple Crown at Belmont. Shit, it's been thirty years since the last Triple Crown winner, Affirmed, in 1978."

"You could be right, my friend," Hutch said. "The one thing these three men have in common is a diabolical hatred of the United States. Even if their dirty trick fizzled, it would scare New Yorkers and the whole country. The attempt at a dirty bomb would bring back memories of 9/11. The story would run on the front pages of every newspaper around the world."

Pete poured the last of the coffee into the three mugs. The enormity of the potential plot they had uncovered could be seen on their grave faces. Each took a sip of the syrupy liquid from the dregs of the coffeepot. The only sound in the room emanated from outside as the waves of the ocean's incoming tide pounded the shore in front of Pete's condo.

"Let's stipulate that what you two are conjuring up is true," Pete said. "Where was the Molly C's ultimate destination? Was she going to pull in at some warehouse dock so they could assemble the device when the storm hit and she was beached? What about the other two bodies fished out of the Halifax river?"

"I think I can put them to rest, so to speak," Manny said. "However, I would feel more confident if we could locate their boat. From what Fred and George have been able to find out, they were just two thugs who probably overheard the word drugs at the café in Miami and thought they could make a quick score. They hijacked, or tried to hijack, the Molly C at the height of the storm, after Pete here answered the mayday call. They killed Anderson and then were swept overboard by the waves."

"I buy your theory, Manny," Hutch said, "but Pete's question, where was John Anderson headed, is key. Also, how did they plan on disposing of the cocaine? My guess is they were going to use the proceeds from selling the stuff to finance their little drama."

"Roger that," Manny said.

"The kind of operation they put together wouldn't take very many players," Hutch conjectured. "They would need a biochemical specialist of sorts, at least someone with knowledge on how to prepare the ricin into finely powdered form for an aerosol-type of dispersal. Anderson filled that position until he was murdered. Someone would have to be in the group who knew how to put together an improvised explosive device, and how to set it off remotely with a cell phone, or some other electronic equipment."

Hutch took a bite out of his sugar-glazed doughnut, washing it down with a sip of coffee. "A small explosive charge could disperse the ricin over a large area," Hutch continued. "Some material would be destroyed by the heat of the explosion, but a relatively small ricin load could still be delivered to a target area. Remember, they probably aren't looking to kill lots of people. They want to scare the country. Their group would also require an aeronautical-type engineer, or sophisticated layman, to launch and guide a drone, more than likely equipped with GPS tracking maps."

Something sharp kept jabbing Hutch in the calf of his leg every time he tried to put his foot around the inside of the chair. He finally stood to check the pocket of his cargo pants and pulled out the laminated marine map he had picked up from the shelf in Anderson's house. "Geez, I forgot I had this map. It was the only thing with writing on it that Pedro didn't scarf up from Anderson's office," Hutch said, throwing the map on the table. "More coffee anyone?" he asked.

"You dumb shit. Look at this map, will ya?" Pete said.

Hutch and Manny leaned over the table to look at the map and then leaned back in their respective chairs and stared at Pete. "Yes...I'll have another cup," Manny said.

"Make that two," Pete said softly. "The coffee filters and coffee can are still on the counter."

"Well, my comrades in arms, it appears our Señor Anderson was headed for Miami, the final destination on Chesapeake Bay, Maryland, with a stop in Daytona Beach. Manny, how many men do you have at Pelican Bay Marina?" Hutch asked as he pushed the button to start the coffeemaker.

"There's around-the-clock surveillance with the knowledge of Ted Adams, the marina's general manager. One of the officers is in uniform on the Molly C. He's out in the open guarding the crime scene, but the rest of the team is undercover. There are two officers, one as a night watchman and the other as a maintenance guy. Adams is unaware his two new employees are cops."

"I suggest you notify the uniformed team guarding the crime scene that their assignment has changed," Hutch said. "In fact, have them make an obvious departure. They can tell Adams they are being called off to another assignment. Let's see if we can draw a member of this dirty little group to the Molly C. No one has taken the bait to contact our friend here. They probably think he's too fat a fish. Who knows about the marina operation in your department, Manny?"

"Fred, George, and Dani know the full story and are involved in the investigation. The undercover officers know about the cocaine and to lookout for anyone inquiring or trying to board the Molly C."

"We three are the only ones who will be privy to the entire operation we map out this morning," Hutch said. "I would also include your three team members, Manny. I've got an operative out of Miami trying to find, and then to track, this Pedro person. However, Pedro's probably already left for the Baltimore get together. If we can find him, maybe he'll lead us to the warehouse. The agency is also tracking down Santiago. He's a mysterious character, doesn't seem to have a home. Pedro is going to have to fly in order to make it to the meeting today. My guess is the word blackout in the blog, refers to no communication of any kind, cell phone, email, or telephone. Hell, maybe they're using carrier pigeons."

Chapter 33

— ••• —

THE TEMPERATURE already registered eighty degrees at one o'clock in the morning. JJ hoped to get a few hours sleep before trying to pick up Pedro's trail. He had flown Hutch to Miami, and after refueling his plane, he immediately headed back to Venezuela. A few hours later, he set the plane down on the farmer's landing strip and fell exhausted on his cot.

"Damn heat. I'm sweating like a pig," JJ grumbled. He had kicked any semblance of the cot's bedding to the floor long ago. JJ repositioned the fan and stopped the oscillation so it blew top speed on his naked body. Feeling a little relief, he fell into a fitful sleep and overslept. Panicked, he sat bolt upright on the narrow cot. A look at the clock indicated otherwise. Now five in the morning, his strategy to find Pedro was percolating along with the coffeepot. He'd go to the Bird's Nest Café down the street from Pablo's. He didn't want to risk Pablo recognizing him if he could help it.

An hour later, JJ sauntered into the café and ordered breakfast. The place was packed with dock workers, but he was lucky to slide onto an empty stool at the counter just before a heavy-set, smelly worker in his fifties sat down. JJ received a curse for his fake out.

The counter girl took his order. She brought back a plate of greasy eggs and bacon and refilled his coffee cup.

"You wouldn't know where I could find a gardener, would you?" JJ asked, peppering his eggs. "I'm looking to buy a place but the yard's a mess."

"No, señor, but you might look up Señora Coco. She worked for John Jackson. He's dead. It was all over the television. Very bad. Very bad. The reporter called him John Anderson, but his real name was Jackson. Anyway, a gardener worked for him. Coco still lives in Jackson's house."

Playing along, JJ asked, "Where do I find this Jackson or Anderson's house?"

"It's not far from here, señor. Just turn right when you leave this café and follow the street along the docks. The house is off this street, up the hill a little, less than a twenty-minute walk I would guess."

"Gracias." JJ finished his greasy eggs, pulled money out of one of his pockets, laying it on the counter.

"Ah, señor, this is your lucky day. Coco just came in. Coco. Coco, come here," the counter girl called out.

"Hey, buenos días. What's up?"

"Coco, this hombre is looking for a gardener. I told him to talk to you. Maybe you can help him being your boss isn't coming back."

"Si, maybe so. Maybe you can buy me breakfast, señor?"

"Coco, you are very bad," the girl chuckled. "There's a table over there next to the kitchen. You two go sit down, and I'll bring your usual, Coco?"

"Si, my usual plus a gooey roll, seeing how this hombre is paying," Coco said, with a raised eyebrow.

"No problem, ladies. Bring me another cup of coffee on your way over, por favor," JJ said.

"So, señor, you're looking for a gardener?" Coco asked.

"Si. I'm looking at a house which is in pretty good shape, but the yard is an eyesore. The gardens are so bad that I may not go through with the deal. I have to find a gardener to clear it out and then restore some of the original plants."

"I think I know someone who could do that. Of course, he is very busy mind you. He would have to work you in. Could cost you, if you know what I mean."

"Coco, if you can find me a competent gardener, I'm sure we could work out a schedule."

"You have a cell phone, señor?"

"Si, Coco," JJ said, pulling his cell out of his pocket. "Do you want me to punch in the numbers?"

"No, señor. I know how," Coco said, a bit offended. She opened the clamshell and carefully hit the numbers and the send button. "Pedro, Coco here. I'm sitting with a man looking for a gardener. I think you might be able to do business, if you know what I mean.

We're eating breakfast at the Bird's Nest Café, his treat....ah...si. Let me ask him." Coco held the phone away from her ear and said to JJ, "Pedro, he's the gardener, said he is getting ready to take a trip. If you can meet him in thirty minutes at his house, you can discuss your business with him."

"Coco, can I get to his house that quickly?"

"Oh, si, señor. It not far from here."

"Then tell him I'll be there in thirty minutes or less."

— • • • —

WITH COCO'S DIRECTIONS, JJ left the café and walked down the street in the direction of Anderson's house. But at the last pier instead of going straight, he turned right onto a small street that climbed the hill in back of Anderson's house. Not far up the hill stood a small stucco house painted in a pale coral. The gardens framing the house were a blaze of colorful flowers, mostly yellow, purple, and corals that matched the house.

JJ walked up to the front porch and raised his hand, but before he could knock the door opened wide. "Señor Pedro?" JJ asked, extending his hand.

"Si. Pedro Riveras. You are Señor JJ?"

"Si. Si. Thank you for meeting me this morning. I'm eager to settle on a house I like but the garden is terrible."

"What house are you considering, señor?"

"It's on the west end of Port of La Gualra, overlooking the water, and you can see the docks. The woman, who showed me the place, said it belonged to a speculator and he wants out. The color of the house is much like yours. Do you know it? It's on Vista Way."

"Si. Si. The man is never there, and that is why the gardens have become overgrown like a jungle. As I told Coco, I'm leaving on a business trip, but I know the property and I think for the right price I can help you. I'll be gone six or seven days. How about you call me next Monday? We can meet at the property and I give you my price. If the garden is the only thing holding you back from putting in an offer, I say go ahead. If we can't come to an agreement, then you can back out before the deal is done. But I think we can work it out."

"If your work is anything like your own garden, then I'm sure we can, too," JJ said. "I have a cab waiting down at the docks. Can I drop you at the airport? You've been kind enough to see me, and you're probably running a little late."

"No. I have a car, but I do have to hurry to get my flight. The Caracas Airport is only thirty minutes away but thank you for the offer."

"Thank you for your time, Pedro. I'll call you next Monday."

JJ retraced his steps and looked for the phantom cab he said was waiting. Fortunately, several cabs, if you could call the dented, scratched and rusty vehicles cabs, were lined up. They were waiting for the cruise-ship passengers to disembark for a few hours of shopping in Caracas. JJ asked the first cabbie in line if he could take him to the airport.

A speed limit must have been nonexistent as the cab raced toward the airport. JJ soon found out that the air conditioning in the cab was definitely non-existent. At the airport, JJ slipped into the men's room and removed his red long-sleeve shirt leaving a white, short-sleeve T-shirt in its place. He pulled a mustache out of one of his cargo pants pockets, a pair of glasses, and a rolled up Red Sox baseball cap. Emerging from the men's room into the throngs of travelers, he headed for the information desk.

"May I help you, señor?" a pretty young Latino woman asked him.

"Si. What flight can you get me leaving in an hour for Miami or Baltimore?"

"You're in luck for Miami, señor. I have an American flight, number 924, scheduled to leave in fifty-five minutes. I see nothing for Baltimore. Perhaps you can get a connection. You can purchase your ticket at the American counter and then go to gate twenty-four."

"Thank you, señorita."

JJ sauntered over to the escalator. At the top of the moving stairs, he ambled as close as he could get to the gate without going through security. He took up a position looking out the large expanse of windows, which acted as a mirror. Within ten minutes, he spotted Pedro pulling a carry-on bag. Pedro went through security and sat in the passenger waiting area for the flight to board for Miami. JJ took Pedro's picture with his cell, left the terminal, and hailed another cab.

He knew he couldn't board the flight and take the chance Pedro would recognize him. The cab dropped him off back at Port of La Guaira. He retrieved his bicycle and rode like a mad man to the plane. Before another trickle of sweat ran down his face, he was airborne and on the phone to the Miami office.

"Hi, Harry. This is JJ. I need some information as fast as your little fat fingers can find it. Yes. Sure. Okay, I owe you dinner, but only if you can get me the following info. American Airline's flight 924 was scheduled to leave Caracas at 10:30 this morning bound for Miami. Did it leave on time, and what time is it scheduled to land? Also, check the flight manifest for a passenger by the name of Pedro Riveras. I'll buy you dessert to go with that dinner if you come up with a connecting flight to Baltimore. I'm in the air now and will set this tanker down at our spot at the Miami airport. One more thing, Harry. If you find this Pedro on that Miami bound flight, be at the arrival area. I'm sending you his picture from my cell. If I don't make it in time, you pick up the tail on him. I think I'll beat the flight, but just in case...okay, a chocolate mudslide."

By JJ's calculation, he figured he'd beat Pedro by fifteen minutes. By the time they let the passengers off the plane, JJ would be in place to pick up the tail.

JJ's plan was working. He raced up to the passenger arrival area and signaled Harry to back off. The two men waited. The last passengers strolled by and then the flight crew. Pedro was nowhere to be seen.

"Shit, I lost him," JJ said, more to himself than anyone else.

Chapter 34

— ••• —

BALTIMORE WAS ABUZZ with teams of media—newspapers, television, and national magazines. All carried a segment on the horse Big Brown. Everyone asked the question, "Can he win the second leg of the Triple Crown, the Preakness?" Betting parlors from Las Vegas to Atlantic City, Dubai to Saudi Arabia were toting up wagers 24/7.

Santiago sat humming, a smile spreading across his face. Thousand-dollar bills danced through his over active imagination. He could see the steward behind the window counting out the money he was going to collect on Saturday.

However, he stifled his excitement by switching to thoughts of the mission he had so meticulously planned. He was not ready to get euphoric over his operation to cause world hysteria until after the test of the drone. They had to be sure that the drone could fly, that the GPS maps were accurate, and that the delivery canister exploded properly when it was triggered by the remote device. All of these issues were to be tested Saturday during the Preakness.

He slowly brought his car to the front gate of a ten-foot high wire fence and stopped. After unlocking the gate, he drove through, locking it behind him. He had installed a buzzer on the inside of one of the iron posts. As his friends arrived for the meeting, they were instructed to press the buzzer. Santiago would come out to open the gate. The blackout on cell phones or any other kind of transmission would remain in effect until the mission was complete—after the Belmont Stakes, and hopefully a Triple Crown winner.

Two times Santiago walked out to open the gate to allow one of his guests to pass through. After the second guest arrived, he asked the two to have a seat so he could update them on his latest recruit.

"Because of the unfortunate demise of our friend John, we are in dire need of another biochemist," Santiago said, clearing his throat. "I went deep into my contacts to find such a person. At first it looked hopeless, and then last week I had a communiqué from a friend of a friend. He knew of a biologist, a specialist in germ warfare. This biologist would like nothing better than to drive the stupid New Yorkers into hysteria, a hysteria that will sweep the country. His name is Christopher Brownhill. He was a chemistry professor at MIT. During his tenure, he gave a lecture at a conference on terrorism. The subject was weapons of mass destruction, the use of ricin in particular."

Santiago paused in his sermon to take a swallow of water to clear his throat.

"Because of the lecture, he came to the attention of the Homeland Security folks. They interviewed him, and Dr. Brownhill was so sure he would be hired that he resigned his teaching post at MIT. The job fell through, and MIT did not want him back. He remained unemployed for three years and now teaches biology at a high school in Vermont. Needless to say, he is very bitter about the way he was treated, both by the university and by Homeland Security. He hates the United States and blames this country for his fall from grace."

"When do we meet this Brownhill?" asked one of Santiago's guests.

"He will be here shortly. I wanted to fill you in before he arrived. Pedro did you bring the bean concoction?" Santiago asked.

"Yes, but it wasn't easy to do in such a rush. There is only a small sample. Maybe Professor Brownhill will have some ideas how to refine the powder so it will be more powerful. I would still like to rescue the good stuff on John's boat. We need money to finance our mission. My supplier balked at giving me anything without more cash. I will need additional funds before we finish the task. Your rules that we are not to fly commercial have drained my bank account. I paid for the commercial flight, and then I had to dig into my pocket again to hire a pilot to fly me to Baltimore from Caracas."

"I, too, would like to get my hands on the Molly C's cargo," said his other guest. "After our test on Saturday, I think we should pursue the idea. The drone, I see, is still under her protective cover over in the corner. I have the fuel in my car. Pedro, is the explosive device ready to be installed? I have the remote control components to set it off. For

Saturday, I created a small banner that will open when Santiago presses the button."

"And what will the banner say?" Santiago asked.

"Go Big Brown."

The three men chuckled, but the smiles ceased suddenly when they heard the buzzer from the fence post. Santiago shuffled out to the gate and escorted Professor Brownhill back to the group.

"Gentlemen, I would like you to meet the fourth member of our team, Professor Christopher Brownhill."

The two other members said they were glad the professor was with them, and the four shook hands.

"Very good," Santiago said. "Now, my friends, let's go over the test for Saturday and then the mission three weeks hence. Let me start with the overall operation. I have rented a storage pod for the drone and our equipment. After Saturday's test, we will pack the pod, and I will drive the truck, with the pod, to New York."

"Where will you put the stuff once you get to New York?" Brownhill asked.

"I have rented a warehouse, a small hangar of sorts, outside of Belmont, New York. I will then return to Caracas. After we pack the pod this Saturday, you all will return to your homes. As we go through preparations for the test, you will each make a list of tools and equipment, with spares, specific to your piece of the plan. There can be no mistakes. There are to be no communications between us unless it is of the utmost urgency, an urgency that would impact the operation. Is that understood?" Santiago looked at each man in turn. Each nodded that he understood.

"We will convene again in New York on Tuesday, June second, five days before the Belmont Stakes, hopefully a race for the Triple Crown. Even if there is no third leg to be won at Belmont, the mission still proceeds. However, I have no doubt that Big Brown will win the Preakness on Saturday. Everything is working perfectly in our favor. The world will be watching."

Chapter 35

—•••—

The Preakness

HUTCH SCHEDULED A MIDNIGHT conference call with Pete and Manny. He alerted the two that his operative lost Pedro in Miami, and they hadn't been able to track down Santiago as yet. Other than that, everything was hunky-dory.

Manny's assignment for the day of the Preakness was to monitor the marina, specifically the Molly C. JJ returned to Port of La Guaira where he hoped to pick up Pedro's trail. Hutch didn't want JJ near the Pimlico race track in case Pedro was there and burned him. Hutch and two other operatives, each equipped with military strength binoculars, would be positioned to watch the sky in all directions from the track's grandstand. Pete would monitor the broadcast of three networks from different angles to see if he spotted anything, or if a network reported a sighting of something unusual.

"Okay," Pete said to himself, hanging up the phone. "Everything is hunky-dory. Now how am I going to sleep?" He turned out the light and closed his eyes. They flew open, his mind racing with bet designs, pilotless aircraft, and a horse named Big Brown. Finally, he dozed off.

—•••—

THE SUN ROSE earlier than usual, or so Pete thought. His nerves were on edge wondering what the day would bring—the running of the Preakness, the second leg of the Triple Crown. Could Big Brown win again? But of prime importance, would he, Pete Peterson from his OTBP, be able to spot a drone flying over Pimlico?

Pete was all thumbs this morning and spilled his morning coffee on his shirt while out on the balcony. "You jerk," he said to himself. "You'd think you'd never been in combat before." He wheeled himself angrily into his bedroom and changed his shirt. He then went to his computer and started his race routine, downloading Santiago's blog. He needed a couple of other handicapper reports, so he started the print job for Santiago—the printer jammed. "Oh boy, one of those days," he cursed. He shut the cranky printer down and queued the remaining documents to his speedy laser machine.

Pete quickly perused Santiago's blog but didn't see anything unusual. The Preakness wasn't scheduled to go off until five in the afternoon, so he had plenty of time to get his nerves under control. He constructed his wagers for the day, but his bet for big money wasn't Santa Anita or any of the other races scheduled at Pimlico. His hope for a significant win was the Preakness Stakes. Big Brown pulled the number seven gate. "Good omen," Pete said. "He's smack dab in the middle of the pack."

An hour before the race was scheduled to run, Pete entered three wagers through his account with the online-betting website. He used the same exotic design he had constructed for the Derby with different horses except for Big Brown.

Still jumpy, he grabbed a bottle of his favorite beer, dumped a bag of tortilla chips on a pizza pan and added some salsa and mozzarella cheese. Popping the concoction into the oven, he set the timer for 5 minutes. While the cheese was melting, he pulled out the sour cream and guacamole. He cleared a spot in front of the middle monitor of his three screens just as the oven timer went off. He retrieved his race day treat from the oven and placed it in front of the monitor. Settling back with his beer and his favorite dish in front of him, he punched in Hutch's cell number and hit the speaker button so he could still nibble his nachos.

"Hey you bastard, don't you know I'm on a stakeout?" Hutch answered.

"Yep, well, while you're out in the sun, your humble servant is ready and waiting for the action, beer in hand, nachos within reach, and nerves as jumpy as a frog who missed his lily pad," Pete replied.

"Next time I see you, remind me to punch you for taking my attention away from the duties of the United States of America," Hutch returned. "By the way, humble servant, anything out of the ordinary in Santiago's blog today?"

"Nope. It was all, shall we say, copacetic."

"Stop with the big words, nacho boy. I'm not impressed."

"I've been watching my monitors off and on most of the day with the pre-race banter, but now my wager is in, my race-treats are in front of me, and the track has my full attention. If something comes across the boob tube, or I spot anything, I'll give you a call. Otherwise, please don't disturb me," Pete said

"Excuse me, bucko. Let me remind you that *you* called me. Over and out." Hutch said.

—•••—

THE SEVENTH RACE, the Preakness Stakes, was set to go. Because Big Brown was expected to win, the odds were very low and wouldn't pay much. It seemed everybody was betting on him to win. It all depended on which horse came in second. The horses were in their cages. The bell rang and the announcer yelled, "They're Off."

Pete leaned forward in anticipation. It didn't matter what the race, his adrenalin always went up when he watched the horses fly out of the gate. The race was nine-and-half furlongs, one and three-sixteenths mile. The eleven horses were packed together. Then at the top of the homestretch, Big Brown swung wide and passed his rivals in a dominating dash to the finish line.

"Who came in second?" Pete yelled. "Who? *Macho Again!* Yahoo! I'm going to win a bundle. Santiago, whoever you are, you're a genius for suggesting Macho Again," Pete said, taking a victory-swig of beer. "Come on. Come on. Show me the payoffs." Staring at the monitor Pete caught a bright spec in the sky, at least he thought he did. He punched in Hutch's number.

"Look to the west, over the parking lot," Pete screamed, before Hutch could say hello.

Sure enough, a large toy plane swooped low over the parking lot.

"Did you see it? Did you see it?" Pete yelled.

"Ya," Hutch said, and the line went dead.

"The bastard hung up on me," Pete muttered.

Swiveling his head from one to the other, Pete continued to look at his monitors. But there were no more shots angled in the direction of the toy plane. None of the announcers referred to the toy. "But, of course, anyone in their right mind would be looking at the track not up in the direction of the parking lot," Pete said talking to himself as usual, "and the plane, of course, couldn't be seen anyway unless you were sitting high up in the stands. Well, Hutch, my fair-weather friend, you may be too busy to talk to me so I'm going to check with Manny. Maybe he saw something."

Pete punched in Manny's cell number. "Hey, Manny, Pete here. Did you see anything? ...no? ...nothing over the parking lot? ...you were looking at the track on ESPN? Well, Mr. Lawman, I saw a toy plane swoop over the parking lot just as the race finished. It let out a banner, *Go Big Brown*."

Chapter 36

— • • • —

"LUCY, I'M HOME," Catherine called to her housekeeper. Her earlier melancholy had dissipated. She was returning from a meeting with Ted Adams. He loved her designs for the marina restaurant and changed very little. He did add some fresh ideas since they first met.

Catherine ran up the two flights of stairs to her studio. She sat down at her architect's table with a fresh tablet of paper. Fishing around in her black leather tote, she pulled out her notes explaining the alterations in the design. They needed to be fleshed out before the ideas slipped away. Catherine buzzed the kitchen intercom, hoping she could catch Lucy before she left for the day.

"Hi, Miss Catherine. What can I do for you?"

"I'm transcribing my notes from a meeting today at the marina. I know you're probably getting ready to leave, but could you fix me a martini before you go? You know how I like it, and a small plate with cheese and crackers? I'm up in the studio."

"You just do your work, Miss Catherine. I'll be up in a jiffy, and I have some messages for you."

Catherine pulled the blueprints out of the tube. She laid them on the counter in the center of her studio moments before Lucy crested the third-floor staircase with her tray of goodies. She set the service down on the glass coffee table in the section designed for client consultations.

"Is there anything else I can do for you, Miss Catherine?"

"There's nothing else, Lucy. It looks wonderful. You said there were messages?"

"Yes, ma'am. Captain Salinas called a couple of hours ago. He said he would call back later, and Mr. Hutch called. He asked if you could ring him on his cell when you got home. He said you had his number."

"Yes, I do. Thanks, Lucy."

Catherine took a sip of the martini and willed herself to come down from her high after the meeting with Ted. She nibbled on a cracker with a piece of sharp cheddar in one hand and her martini in the other as she walked around the blueprint designs on the counter. Ted enlarged the dining room to accommodate a wall-of-water effect on one end. She wanted to get right to work designing the feature. She told him it was a wonderful idea and would lend such a nice ambiance to his patrons' dining experience.

The phone rang, cutting into her thoughts. She laid the half-eaten cracker on the counter and punched the speaker button on her phone so she could continue to enjoy her martini and crackers.

"How's the most beautiful woman in Port Orange today?" Hutch asked before she finished saying hello.

"I can tell you this woman on the phone is very excited," she answered.

"I'm not sure I want to hear that—very excited when I'm not the one causing this excitement. I'm up here in my townhouse, beer in hand, unhappy, wishing I was there with you. What makes you so bubbly?"

"I just had a wonderful, stimulating meeting with a client. He loved my new design for his restaurant, and he came up with a feature that is going to make it spectacular."

"Wow, you are excited and now stimulated? Who is this client?"

"He's Ted Adams. He manages Pelican Bay Marina," Catherine said.

Silence filled the line between them.

"Hutch, are you there? I said I met with—"

"I heard you. That's the marina where the Molly C is being stored, the boat that beached during that bad storm. You know, you honored Daytona Pete at the auction a couple of weeks ago."

"Oh, yes it is. I should have asked Ted about the boat and what he's going to do with it. It totally slipped my mind that the Molly C was there. Actually, for all I know, someone may have claimed it."

"Catherine, I don't think you should be going over to that marina."

"For heaven's sake, why not? Why would you say such a thing? Why aren't you excited for me?" Catherine said, her bubble of excitement bursting. She took a long sip of her martini, trying to tamp down the irritation she felt rising.

"You know Manny found a body on that boat. A body, I might add, that was shot in the head. In other words, the man was murdered," Hutch said. He could feel himself growing angry. How was he going to keep her away from the marina? His gut told him it was a dangerous place.

"Yes, I know about the murdered man. It was on the news, but the boat was found beached in New Smyrna. I think it's just being stored at the marina until they can figure out who owns it. I really don't appreciate your telling me what to do. I'm a professional meeting with a client on a job, a very big job, I might add. You're treating me like a child." Catherine took another long sip of her martini. Her mood had switched from irritation to anger. "What are you trying to tell me, Mr. Hutchinson? If you think it's dangerous, then explain why. Otherwise knock off the big brother act. You can't shelter me from going about my business," Catherine retorted.

"God knows I'm not your big brother. If I think you shouldn't go some place, I'll tell you so."

"Great. You go traipsing off to God knows where. I have no idea if you are likely to be killed, and yet you want me to stay locked up in my house? Well, it's not going to happen. You've said your work kept getting in the way of a relationship with a woman. Well, now I can see why. It's a good thing this happened so we can end it now. If you'll excuse me, I want to get back to the restaurant design while the ideas are still fresh. Goodbye," Catherine said angrily and hung up.

"My temper generally doesn't come to the surface, but when it does, watch out, Mr. Hutchinson. You have some nerve, telling me I can't go to the marina" she muttered, draining the last of her drink. The martini and her excitement were gone.

Chapter 37

—•••—

"WOMEN," HUTCH SAID TO HIMSELF. "Whoever said you can't live with them, and you can't live without them sure was right. Just face it, Hutch old boy, she got to you. You're supposed to be this big government agent, so why don't you solve the problem? Well, maybe I'll do just that," he said, pacing around his house like a caged lion. "I have to go to Daytona Beach anyway. Why not do it now? You sure as hell aren't going to sleep tonight, big guy."

Hutch called Andrews Air Base and learned a government plane bound for Miami was leaving in forty-five minutes. If he could get to Andrews before it left, the crew would be glad to let him off at the Daytona Beach Airport.

Three-and-a-half hours later, he stood on Catherine's doorstep, wondering what he was going to say to her. What he was going to say didn't matter as much to him as being able to hold her in his arms and never let her go again.

He was leaning on his raised arm against the door frame, loosening his tie with the other hand, when Lucy opened the door.

"Agent Hutch, what a surprise. Miss Catherine didn't tell me she was expecting you. Come in please," Lucy said. "She's up in her studio working late I guess. Please tell her I'm leaving now, but I'll be back first thing in the morning. Have a nice evening."

"Thank you, Lucy. I'll tell her."

Hutch took the stairs two at a time. Hitting the landing on the third floor, he came to an abrupt halt. Catherine was perched on a stool at the blueprint counter, a glass of wine in one hand and a wadded-up tissue in the other. She seemed to be staring without seeing what was on the blueprint in front of her. To Hutch she looked miserable, and it broke his heart to think that he was probably the cause.

"Catherine," he whispered softly.

Startled, she looked up. A fresh tear meandered down her cheek as she stood rooted to the floor.

"My beautiful, sweet Catherine. My angel," Hutch mumbled, as he strode to her, encased her in his arms. His hand on her back pressed her against him. His other hand stroked her hair as he eased her head onto his chest.

"Hutch, I'm so sorry. I said such stupid things."

"My darling, I'm the one who should apologize for being such an overbearing fool," he said, pulling his handkerchief from his pocket, softly dabbing her beautiful brown eyes. "Catherine, the thought of not seeing you or being with you, I—" the end of the sentence was lost as he softly kissed her lips, her eyes, and her lips again. The kiss deepened sending heat throughout his body. He wanted her, all of her. She wilted into his arms. He picked her up, carried her to the couch, gently laying her down on the soft plush cushions.

Kneeling beside her, he felt a quiver ripple up her body. He pulled her to him. Slowly he pulled two of the throw pillows down to the floor and again gently lowered her from the couch to the pillows. Now he could cradle her, kiss her. Her temperature was mounting. He could feel it on her skin.

"Catherine, I love you. I'd die if I couldn't see you, if I couldn't hold you like this, if I lost you."

"Hutch, I thought I'd pushed you away. My sweetheart...I love you, too."

Her loose silk black shirt conformed to the shape of her breasts, rising and falling with each breath. Sliding his hand up under the silk, he caressed her soft skin. The scent of her perfume was intoxicating. Moaning, he kissed her again, deeper, tasting the sweetness of her mouth.

"Touch me, sweetheart. Love me," she begged.

He unbuttoned her shorts, sliding them down her long bronze legs. "Catherine, you're so beautiful," he said, as he slowly pulled her panties off over her delicate feet, revealing her exquisite body. He was overcome with the vision of her—her body anxiously waiting to receive him. "Catherine, I have nothing with me to protect you. Do you want me to stop?"

"No. No. Don't stop, my sweetheart. Please don't stop. It's all right."

Hutch didn't make love to her, he devoured her. The silk tank top was gone and Catherine's body was his and his was hers.

—•••—

THEY LAY IN each other's arms, not being able to move, nor wanting to move for fear the moment would end. Hutch rolled to his side pulling her over against him, her body snuggling into the crook of his arm.

"I hope I wasn't too rough, my darling. I couldn't get enough of you. I wanted everything all at the same time." He lifted her chin, gently kissed her bruised lips. "I meant what I said, Catherine Hainsworth. I love you. I'm not sure what we're going to do about it, but I'll do everything I can to be with you. I can't say that I won't be protective of you, but I'll try to help you understand, if I am. If you still tell me to back off, I will, but I won't be very far away."

"I can't believe how wonderful I feel," Catherine said, "after the dreadful way this evening started. We both must understand why the quarrel happened—that awful phone call. For now, I'm content to lie pressed next to you with no space between us, real or imaginary."

"Catherine, I want to see you. Hell, I want to be with you, but you must understand that I can't read you into my missions. Knowing where I am and what I'm doing could put you in danger. I would break my oath, jeopardize the mission, my team could be killed, and you could be killed. Can you accept that part of my life, knowing I will not be able to share my work with you?"

Untangling herself from his arms, Catherine slowly sat up, so did Hutch. She draped the throw blanket from the couch around her. They both knew the conversation was touching on a serious and emotional subject.

Still on the floor, she leaned back against the couch, gazing into his eyes. "I'd like to say I could, and I will try very hard, but I was really upset when you almost forbade me from doing my job at the marina. I guess I should ask for a compromise. If you can't tell me why then give me some options. This is a big job. I'm very involved and can't, no, let's say I don't want to walk away. If I did walk away, I'd have to give a reason for quitting. That would raise more questions, perhaps questions you might not want me to ask. Questions you couldn't answer."

"Can you do this? Whenever you go to the marina, please do it as a scheduled meeting and let me know you're going. That way, you can do your job, and I can watch your back, so to speak, which is a great idea. I love your back," he said, leaning in and giving her lips a brush.

"I'll try." Getting up off the floor, tucking the blanket around her like a bath towel, she went over to her desk. "I have something for you." Opening the center drawer, she picked up a small box and returned to sit by Hutch again. "I bought this for you after our visit in Washington."

Hutch took the small box and untied the gold metallic ribbon. Inside he carefully picked up a gold St. Christopher medal, the size of a nickel but oval in shape. The rim was trimmed in black onyx.

"I'll carry this forever knowing you are with me," he said. "You and I seem to think alike." He leaned over to grasp his trousers. Putting his hand in the right-front pocket, he withdrew a white box exactly the size Catherine had given him. It was tied with a silver ribbon. "I, too, bought this after our visit in Washington that ended so abruptly."

Catherine untied the ribbon and opened the box. Inside she found a round gold St. Christopher medal with a delicate gold chain. The exquisite medal was the size of a dime. The border around the saint appeared as if made of fine lace.

"Oh, Hutch, it's beautiful," she said, putting the chain around her neck as he helped her close the clasp. "I'll wear it close to my heart…treasure it always."

—•••—

THE NEXT MORNING Hutch woke with a start. He eased back against the pillow as the memory of the night filled his senses, the memory of holding Catherine and making love to her until they both were sated. He reached for her just as the aroma of freshly brewed coffee hit his brain. Pulling on his shirt and trousers, he made his way down to the kitchen.

"Now there is a sight for sore eyes. The most beautiful woman in the world about to pour two cups of coffee," he said, fishing his arms through her robe and holding her close. She lifted her face to meet his lips.

"Hey, Agent Hutchinson," she said, pulling away with a smile. "Lucy's here. Whatever will she think of us?"

"That we're in love, my angel. That we're in love."

Chapter 38

—•••—

HUTCH PULLED INTO PETE'S parking garage. He wasn't sure how he got there because his mind was consumed with Catherine. He wanted to be with her every minute. Anytime away from her was torture. "So what are you going to do about it?" he asked. "I know what I want to do." He continued talking to himself as he got off the elevator and pushed Pete's doorbell. "But would it be fair to her?"

Pete opened his door and caught the last two words. "Who are you talking to or have you gone psycho on me?" Pete asked as he rolled a few inches into the hall. He looked left and right, but no one was there. Backing up into his condo, he motioned Hutch to go in. He left the door ajar for Manny and Peaches to join the team meeting.

"Shut up, shithead, and get me some coffee. I'm exhausted," Hutch said.

"Okay, okay, and why is that, or should I ask who was she? As if I didn't know."

"Just get me the damn coffee."

"Okay. Okay. You don't have to bite my head off," Pete said, grinning. "It must have been some night. You look beat."

Peaches bolted in through the partially open door making a bee-line for Pete. He saw her coming, but he wasn't quick enough in setting the full coffee cup down on the counter. Some of the liquid hit her head, partially covering Pete's shorts as well. The balance of the coffee hit the floor. Peaches shook her head spraying the remnants onto Pete's shirt.

"Geez, Peaches, calm down will ya?" Pete said, wiping his shirt with a paper napkin.

Hutch grabbed a kitchen towel and started to mop up the floor.

"Give me that thing," Pete said, laughing. "My shirt and Peaches' head need to be mopped up more than the damn floor. Don't we, girl? I'll say this for you, Peaches, that was a helluva greeting. Pardon me gentlemen, Peaches and I have to go change my shirt," he said, rolling into the bedroom.

"Hutch, if you know how to work that coffeemaker, I suggest you put on a fresh pot," Manny said brusquely. "I'll get the easel. There's a lot we have to go over."

Pete rolled out of the bedroom with Peaches trotting behind, then to her favorite spot at the sliding-glass doors. She took up her position monitoring the diving pelicans.

"Well, don't we look pretty?" Hutch said to Pete. "Nice horsy on your shirt, and if I'm not mistaken, that looks similar to Big Brown."

"Now don't go getting on my case. It is not *similar*. It *is* Big Brown."

"With fans like you, UPS must be making a fortune," Hutch said.

"Okay, you two. Can we get to work here? I have more to do today than to watch you guys spar. But I have to say the first round goes to Peaches."

Hearing her name, Peaches dusted the floor with her tail but didn't look over because the bird traffic outside had her full attention.

Hutch poured everyone a fresh cup of coffee. Manny fished out the half-and-half from the refrigerator as Hutch grabbed a marker and moved to the easel.

"Here's what we know," Hutch said. "The Belmont Stakes, AKA Triple Crown, is two-and-a-half weeks away on a Saturday. Are we in agreement, at least until something changes, that we appear to be dealing with an unaffiliated group of terrorists who seem to have a gripe against the United States?"

Pete and Manny nodded in agreement, both taking sips of their coffee.

"Santiago is connected to Pedro, who was connected to John Anderson. John Anderson captained the Molly C from Port of La Guaira to Miami and was beached in New Smyrna. Given the map I found at his house, let's also assume he was headed for Daytona Beach. Both Miami and Daytona Beach were circled on the map along with Port of La Guaira."

Hutch topped off his coffee, took a sip, and moved back to the easel.

"Pete's interception of the code on Santiago's blog indicated the Preakness was a test target. Pete saw a drone-like object fly in low over Pimlico's parking lot at the end of the eighth race, the Preakness. The drone flew by remote control."

"What about the payload?" Manny asked.

"A timer was set, or someone triggered the banner to unfold—Go Big Brown. We also know that after the coded paragraph in the blog was displayed, Pedro was on the move. My operative found Pedro and tailed him as far as Miami. Let me amend that statement. He tailed Pedro to the Caracas airport and the gate for a flight to Miami. Bottom line, my operative lost Pedro. Are we okay so far?" Hutch asked.

"Yes," Manny agreed, "but let's add we found 216 pounds of cocaine and a cup of ricin under the bed on the Molly C. Also the marina's under surveillance."

Hutch added the surveillance to the first page of the easel pad. He also wrote John Anderson/Jackson at the bottom and after the name wrote "biologist." He flipped the pad to a blank sheet.

"Now, here's what we don't know. Can three men—a dead biologist, a gardener, and an ex-jockey, now handicapper—pull off such a sophisticated plan to trigger a mist of ricin over a race track and potentially wipe out thousands of people?"

The room fell silent. The crashing of the waves below the balcony was the only sound in the room. The enormity of what they faced searing into their very beings.

Pete was the first to break the silence. "Each aspect of the plan is not hard. It's the coordination and timing that ups the ante. Also, it takes money, not only for equipment, drone parts as well as the delivery device, but payment to buy some of the talent they're missing. After all, they don't have Anderson, the biologist, anymore. And, they don't have the coke, if they planned to use the proceeds from selling the bricks to fund this little game they're playing."

"Hutch, flip back to the first page," Manny said. "Under Anderson, add the tattoo. Dani thinks it's a condor, a vulture type of bird. It may be nothing but add it anyway."

Hutch flipped to the first page and noted Manny's comment. He then skipped to a fresh sheet and wrote "Assignments" at the top. "We have to find Pedro and Santiago fast. Surveillance of their activities is crucial. Let me reiterate, gentlemen, we have no concrete evidence of a crime beyond the murder of John Anderson with a bullet hole through his head, and drugs found on his boat. My office is working the drug issue in Venezuela. As soon as I know anything, you'll be informed."

"We also have possession of the drugs," Manny stated.

Hutch dragged his hand over his hair, looked down at the floor in concentration, then looked back up at Pete and Manny. "I say we try a new approach to lure them out to recover their bricks. You can bet that someone besides Anderson knows the stuff was secured in a specially made compartment of the bed. Manny, pull the officers standing watch over the crime scene and change the assignment to undercover surveillance. Ted Adams won't be aware they're still around, and you believe he doesn't know his two new employees are undercover cops. Put the Molly C back in the water but still moored at the marina. Issue a press release saying no one has claimed the boat, so it's going up for sale in, say, ten days."

"I like it, Hutch. What do you think, Manny?" Pete asked.

"It could flush them out. They have to be hurting for cash," Manny replied.

"Remember, if it wasn't for that storm, they would be in hog heaven pulling off the greatest terrorist act since 9/11. Bastards," Pete uttered, under his breath.

"Exactly," Hutch said. "The agency picks up all kinds of chatter from known groups. It's the errant, disillusioned, America haters operating under our radar that are so scary."

Hutch turned back to the assignment list. "My office is tracking down Pedro and Santiago. Manny, you get the Molly C in the water, put out the press release that she's for sale, and monitor the surveillance team. I hope to God we flush someone out. Time is not in our favor. Pete, do you have a shredder?"

"Yup, over in the corner. I'll take care of your scribbles."

"Okay, I'm out of here," Hutch said. "I'm hopping a plane back to Washington as soon as I can get to Daytona Beach Airport. Keep your cell phones charged and on you at all times. Thanks for the coffee, Pete."

"Yep, and thanks for the doughnuts. Not." Pete countered.

"Oh shit, I'm sorry. I was running a little late. I owe you." Hutch gave Pete a friendly sock on the shoulder and headed for the door. Manny and Peaches were right behind him, riding down the elevator together. Heading for his car, Hutch called back to Manny.

"Manny, I want to alert you to keep a watch out for Catherine."

"What are you talking about?" Manny asked, irritated, his voice gruff.

"She's doing a big job for Pelican Bay Marina. Ted Adams asked her to design a new dining room on the river side of the building. I guess it will just about double the size of his operation. I've asked her to let me know when she has a meeting there, and when she returns home, or to the office at Stone & Associates."

"Why call you? I'm here in Daytona Beach. Why wouldn't she let me know?"

"No reason, I just happened to be talking to her when she told me about the job," Hutch said.

"Well, do you have a problem if I ask her to let me know instead?" Manny countered.

"Yes, I do have a problem with that. How about if she lets us both know?" Hutch shot back.

"Fine. I'll call her and ask her to let us *both* know." Manny said clearly annoyed.

Stepping off the elevator and walking out of the condo building each man turned in separate directions.

Hutch called the airport to confirm his plane was ready to go. The tower verified it was. Then he called Catherine. "Hi, beautiful."

"Hello, sweetheart. It feels like days since you left this morning."

"I know. You're all I can think about."

"When will I see you again?" she asked.

"I'm on my way to the airport, and I expect to be gone a few days. If there is any way possible, I'll be back to you by Friday. In the meantime, please remember I love you."

"I love you, too, my darling."

The line went silent, neither one wanted to break the connection. Hutch pulled into the airport's car rental return and reluctantly shut off his phone.

Chapter 39

—•••—

THE HOMELAND SECURITY JET rose leaving the Daytona Beach Airport behind. The sky was light blue with an occasional cloud drifting by. Hutch banked the plane to the north toward Washington when his cell beeped. A staffer informed him they had learned that Luis Santiago had a piece of real estate in Caracas. They had yet to verify if he had a home there. JJ was in Port of La Guaira waiting for Pedro to return.

"Tell JJ, I'm on my way to Caracas. Ask him to let me know the minute he sees Pedro," Hutch ordered. "Also tell him I'll refuel in Miami. Then I'll be landing on our little strip, so he needs to move his aircraft out of my way." He reversed his course, heading south. A plan to find Santiago forming in his head.

Several hours later, he set the plain white aircraft, with two blue stripes painted on each side, down onto the farmer's brush-dotted runway. *This operation better wrap up soon or the natives are going to report us,* he thought.

JJ ducked under the wing just as Hutch swung the door open. "We have to stop meeting like this, partner," JJ said, giving his friend a bear hug.

"Any sight of Pedro?" Hutch asked.

"Nothing. I'm getting a little tired hanging out at the Bird's Nest Café. Coco assures me he'll return at anytime. How does she know? Maybe she's psychic. Let's get out of this heat. I want to hear your plan to find Santiago."

The two went over to JJ's aircraft. Hutch's plane wasn't outfitted with the basic living paraphernalia, such as cots, refrigerator, or a shower.

"I'm heading to Hotel Catimar," Hutch said, unscrewing the cap of an icy cold beer. "I'm told the hotel is five minutes from the Caracas airport. There's a subway connecting downtown Caracas with the airport and Port of La Guaira. My plan is to go to La Rinconada Horse

Track tomorrow. They only race Saturday and Sunday afternoon, but I'm hoping to glean some information on Santiago in the track's barn area. By the way, watch out for Coco. She may want your number in more ways than one."

"Shut up, you wise ass. Don't worry about me, you watch out for your sorry specimen of a body. However, to show you how much I care about your well being, I bought us a couple of motorcycles. Peddling a bicycle down to the waterfront was getting tiresome."

"Hey, good idea. Thanks for the beer. I'm going to head out so I can get to the hotel before nightfall. Don't forget, it's critical we keep in touch with each other."

Hutch mounted one of the motorcycles and rode down to the waterfront. He went into Pablo's and asked him if he would keep an eye on his bike for a couple of days. Pablo was more than happy to oblige when Hutch greased his palm with a fifty-dollar bill. The subway station was easy to find, and within an hour he had registered at the hotel, enjoying the coolness of his room. He decided what he needed was a steak dinner and good night's sleep. Room service would do nicely. The hotel reportedly had a five-star rating, so how bad could the food be?

Chapter 40

— • • • —

THE MEETING WITH HUTCH and Pete had been alarming, but it wasn't the meeting that upset Manny. He was annoyed at Hutch, and he was annoyed at himself for being annoyed. He pulled into traffic gunning the motor a little more than usual. Peaches lost her footing, sliding against the door. She righted herself and Manny reached over to give her a pat. They continued on to the department without further incident.

Manny was still off kilter learning that Hutch told Catherine to call him and not Manny whenever she went to Pelican Bay Marina. "It's in my jurisdiction," he said to himself. "I'm in charge in Daytona Beach." Of course, he realized the real reason for his irritation was he feared Catherine might become involved with Hutch, and once again she would be out of his reach.

Manny stomped into the bullpen with a scowl on his face. Fred, George, and Dani looked up when they heard him. Each of them noticed his bad mood and said in unison, "Hi, Manny." The three turned back to their computer screens, intent on whatever was displayed. Peaches went up and nudged Dani's elbow, hoping for one of the secret treats she kept in the drawer. Peaches didn't have to wait long. She took the bone-shaped biscuit to her pillow, and after a couple of crunches swallowed the beefy tasting morsel.

"Dani," Manny said, in a stern voice.

"I know. I know. I'm sorry, but the biscuit was very small, and she asked me so sweetly I couldn't resist."

"Okay, everybody. Let's get down to business," Manny said.

The three team members turned off their monitors and swiveled to face Manny, hoping for some news in the case.

"We have to move faster. Time is running out. There are only seventeen days until the Triple Crown, and we don't know where the bastards are. I'm reading the three of you in on all aspects. None of the information, I repeat, *none* of the information goes beyond the three of you unless you clear it with me first. Is that understood?"

The three nodded in agreement. Dani picked up her half-empty coffee cup, looking expectantly over the brim at her boss.

"So far you know we have two undercover officers working in maintenance at the marina. Their assignment is to watch for any suspicious activity around the Molly C. They also know drugs were found on board and as far as they are concerned, the stuff is still there. That's all they know. They know nothing about the ricin." Manny filled them in on the intercepted code in Santiago's blog and everything else that was discussed at the meeting with Pete and Hutch.

"We have the task of trying another method to draw out the terrorist gang, this time using the Molly C as bait. When we're finished here, Fred, you pull off the officers watching the Molly C as a crime scene. The officer presently on duty is to remove all the yellow tape. Then I want you and George to head up round-the-clock under-cover surveillance. Use officers you pull from the detail to fill out the schedule. Remember, a gang member may be watching so be careful you aren't burned. As far as they know, the drugs were never discovered."

"Okay, but what's the new plan?" Fred asked.

"I'm going to pay a visit to Adams and tell him we're releasing the Molly C. She goes back in the water at the marina with a For Sale sign on her. $250,000 is the price, but negotiable. I'm putting out a press release stating the Molly C will be sold in five days at a bargain price. Anyone interested is to call the marina."

Manny pulled a bottle of water from his desk drawer, unscrewed the top, and took a long swallow.

"George, let our two guys working for Adams know of the change in plans as far as the yacht going up for sale. They are aware of the drug angle," Manny said, "but not, I repeat, *not* the ricin aspect. Tell them to keep alert and report any activity immediately. I don't care if somebody sneezes, they are to let us know if it looks suspicious. Dani, here are the main points for the press release. Draft it up. After I give the okay, get it to your contact at Channel 13. Buy air time for several spots and ask them to air it immediately and on a rotating schedule over the next few days until notified otherwise. Also get the press release to the *News Journal*. That's it. Get to it everybody."

Manny called Adams. He told Ted he was within a couple of blocks of the marina and wanted to see him for a minute. Ten minutes later, he and Peaches arrived at the marina and found Ted in his office.

"Hi, Ted. No no, don't get up, this will only take a few minutes," Manny said. "We're putting the Molly C up for sale. I believe we have all the evidence we're going to get from her. She's just costing the city money to keep her in dry-dock at your marina. So, as soon as you and your men can get her into the water the better. I'd like you to put a For Sale sign in her bow window. Do you have a bulletin board where you can post a press release?"

"Yes. There's one in the lounge," Ted replied.

"Good. Here are a few copies of the release we're giving to Channel 13. It should be on the air in a couple of hours. It will also appear in the morning edition of the *News Journal*. You can use the press release for the bulletin board. Here's another copy for the boat's window. The sale will take place in five days, and she goes to the highest offer. It could turn into an auction situation with more than one bidder. We're asking $250,000. What do you think of the price?" Manny asked.

"She's a beauty, very sleek, powerful, and in good condition from what I saw when she was beached. Because of your department's yellow crime-scene tape, I haven't had a chance to look her over inside. It sounds like a good deal. Is there room for negotiation, or is the price fixed?"

"Hey, Ted, there's always room for negotiation," Manny replied, chuckling. "If all goes well, she should be off your hands soon. We appreciate your taking care of her."

"No problem, Manny. I'll see that my boys have her in the water this afternoon. We'll tie her up at the end of our last dock so potential buyers can look her over without getting in the way of my other boat owners," Ted said, getting out of his chair to escort Manny out to the front door of the marina.

"The officer standing watch will have the yellow tape off her within the hour. Thanks again, Ted, for your help," Manny said, shaking Ted's hand. He let Peaches out of the car and walked over to take a look at the Molly C. "Peaches, old girl, let's hope this flushes out the bad guys," he said, absentmindedly stroking her silky head. Peaches walked a little closer to him so he could reach her better.

— • • • —

CHANNEL 13 AIRED the information of the upcoming sale of the Molly C by mid-afternoon. Dani asked them to air it every two to three hours. With all the boaters in the area, the sale of the yacht at $250,000 was a steal. The next morning, below the fold of the front section, there was a small article with a picture of the beached boat stating it was to be sold. A longer article appeared on the first page of the sports section.

Manny was having lunch at his desk when Fred walked into the bullpen. "Hey, if I'd known you were going out for a sandwich you could have picked one up for me," Fred told him, sitting down in his chair. He eagerly pulled out his Rueben sandwich with an extra dill pickle.

"Anything from your surveillance men?" Manny asked.

"Nope. All is quiet on the waterfront."

"Damn, I hope this works, "Manny said, between bites. "If it doesn't, I'm not sure we can stop these shitheads in time—"

The ring from Fred's cell phone interrupted Manny. "What?" Fred shouted, shooting to his feet. He turned to Manny. "It's Tony Sullivan, our guy working for Adams. Give that to me again. Real slow from the top…okay…okay…hold on. Shit, he hung up," Fred said, snapping his cell shut.

"What's up?" Manny barked. He could tell by Fred's actions that whatever Tony said wasn't good.

"Adams sold the Molly C. The new owner didn't seem to know a bow from a stern, but he wanted to get the yacht out to sea and down to his own dock right away. Tony was untying her lines when the guy yelled at him. He asked Tony if he wanted to make a fast C-note. He'd pay Tony if he'd drive the darn thing for him. He wasn't going too far so he said Tony could be back to work by morning."

"You're shittin me, Fred," Manny yelled, punching in Ted's number. "Hey, Ted, any nibbles on the Molly C yet? …you what? …you sold her? No, Ted's that's not great. The sale was supposed to be in five days…I don't care if you got the full price and I don't care that you got cash. Who bought her?" Manny asked.

Manny paced furiously around the bullpen as he talked with Adams. Peaches was standing at attention with a low gurgle in her throat. She was ready to attack as soon as her master gave the signal who to go after.

"Shit, Ted, I know I said I was releasing her, and it's great you sold her." With all the will power he could muster, Manny lowered his voice and forced a calmness he didn't feel. His whole body was ready to spring. "Well, good for you, Ted. Who bought her?" Manny asked, again. He took a deep breath, closed his eyes and hoped to God Ted gave him a name.

"Charles Bromley? From Atlanta?" Manny said. "Well, isn't that nice. What? What was that? One of your maintenance guys is on board? He called to let you know the new owner needed help getting to Ft. Lauderdale, and he should be back in the morning? Well, doesn't that beat all? That's what I call service. Thanks, Ted."

Manny hung up the phone and charged around the bullpen. He jabbed a fist into the palm of his hand. He jabbed his palm again—his sandwich forgotten.

"That goddamn son-of-a-bitch sold the boat. Adams said why wait five days when he had the full price, cash in hand? I guess I can't blame him, but what a mess that puts our operation in. Any more from Tony?" Manny growled.

"No, and I don't think we should call him. He's a good officer, Manny. He thinks the stuff is still on board so you can bet he'll keep us updated. Hell, he could even make sergeant if he plays his cards right."

"I can't believe you're thinking about promoting a guy when the city of New York is at stake. It's not far from Belmont you know—"

A beep from Fred's cell cut into Manny's tirade. "Hey, just a minute, I'm getting a text message from Tony," Fred said. "He says to eat my heart out. He and Bromley are enjoying a beer together. He thought I might enjoy a picture of the new owner sunning himself on the stern deck."

"That's it? A text message? Where'd you get this idiot?"

"Yes, dumb like in Einstein. Look at this picture?" Fred said.

"Give me your damn phone. Let me see the guy who just put thousands of people in harm's way. Wait a minute. Fred, do you see what I see? He has a tattoo on his left arm. It's identical to Anderson's."

Chapter 41

—•••—

FOLLOWING A FITFUL NIGHT'S SLEEP, Hutch hailed a cab and headed to the race track in Caracas. After an altercation with the cabbie about his outrageous fare, the two finally settled on an amount. *Maybe he's just cranky because of the heat and humidity,* Hutch thought, walking away from the cab and heading to the track entrance.

Unsuccessful in obtaining directions to the barn from an attendant, he tucked a twenty-dollar bill into the sweaty palms of some men who played like they were the most important employees at the track. Following several different directions from the entrance, through the stands, and past shuttered food huts, he finally entered the barn area. Only a few horses were in the stalls. It was too early in the week for the animals to arrive for the coming weekend's meet.

Hutch asked a couple of the barn hands if they knew where he could find Santiago. They knew of him but hadn't seen him, much less have a clue whether he lived in Caracas.

Then he got lucky.

A stable hand took a wrinkled picture out of his shirt pocket. "Si, señor. I know him. Here is Santiago and me. I keep it close to my heart so maybe someday I can be like him."

Hutch slowly took the picture from his hand. The man he called Santiago was only a head taller than the boy. He appeared short even for a jockey. In the picture, Santiago was wearing a tank top, long pants, and sandals on his feet.

"When was this taken, son?" Hutch asked.

"A few months ago. The big man came to the barn to check one of the horses in the next day's race. It was very hot so he took a quick shower. I was lucky to be outside the shower, and a friend took this picture. Good, no?" the boy asked excited.

"Very good. Mind if I take a picture of it so I can show you and Santiago together to my friends?"

"Si, señor. You go ahead. Maybe it will bring me luck to become a famous jockey."

"Do you know where Santiago lives? Near here perhaps?" Hutch asked.

"No. Not here, señor. But not far. He lives in a big house in the city. I drive by sometimes and dream that maybe one day I'll have a big house like his."

"You keep riding and I bet you will. What is your name, son?" Hutch asked.

"Roberto, señor. Roberto Santos."

"Roberto, if I buy you some lunch, could you show me where Santiago lives?"

"Ah, si, señor. Maybe you could give me a tip, if I show you, por favor?"

"That depends, Roberto. Do you have a car you drive to this track?"

"Si, señor, I drive you. Then you give me a very big tip?" Roberto asked with a toothy grin.

Roberto gave Hutch a grand tour in his beat-up Chevy of some of the neighborhoods. He wound around the streets pointing out sights he thought his new friend might find interesting. At Hutch's urging, he finally drove by Santiago's house. It wasn't as grand as Roberto led Hutch to believe. The gold stucco building sported a typical red-tile roof. The garden was quite beautiful and Hutch could make out an interior patio through an archway flanked with feathery palm fronds. He made note of the address and then asked Roberto if he would drop him off at the airport. Roberto agreed after receiving two one-hundred dollar bills for his trouble. Hutch thought maybe Roberto would now have enough money for his lunch.

At the airport, Hutch boarded the subway heading back to Port of La Guaira. He called JJ to let him know he'd be joining him at the plane within the hour. JJ was sitting in the shade of the plane's wing when Hutch rode up.

"You'll never guess what I have on my cell," Hutch said.

"Hmmm, a rash from crawling around the horse barn?"

"Shut up and look at this. I have a picture of Santiago and he appears to have a tattoo on his left arm just below the shoulder. The tattoo isn't very distinct because the picture is at an angle, but I swear it looks identical to the one on John Anderson's arm. Unless you caught Santiago without a shirt, even a shirt with short sleeves, you'd never know he had a tattoo."

"Was he home?" JJ asked taking a look at the picture on Hutch's cell.

"No. But once I had the address, I was able to get his telephone number," Hutch said, digging out a crumpled piece of paper from his pocket. "Here it is. Get in touch with your office in Miami. Tell them we need manpower for two round-the-clock undercover surveillance teams, one for Pedro and one for Santiago. We need crackerjack agents at tailing. You are to be in charge of the teams. When they get here, be sure to impress upon them the importance of the tail. They *can't* lose them."

"Well, Mr. Smarty Pants," JJ said, "while you were out playing with the horsies, your pal Manny called. His big news was that the Molly C was sold, and you'll never guess who it was sold to."

"Who?" Hutch asked, looking directly at JJ.

"A guy with a tattoo just like the one in that picture of Santiago."

"Their plot is beginning to fall around their sweet terrorists' asses. Did Manny say anything more—what did this guy do after he bought the boat? Where did he go? Are they tailing him? Come on, man, give."

"It came down in a convoluted way, but yes, the boat and the new owner are under very close surveillance. Give Manny a call, and he'll fill you in," JJ said. "I warn you, some of his language gets pretty explicit. Seems Ted Adams didn't exactly follow Manny's instructions for how the sale was to be handled."

—•••—

THE DAY HAD BEEN long but very productive. Hutch stepped out of the plane. The stars were out, and the bullfrogs were calling their mates. *Thank the good Lord for cell phones,* he thought. He could call Catherine without blowing his location, but he'd have to keep his call short. No chance for questions. With luck, he'd be holding her in his arms soon. He punched in her code and waited impatiently for her to pick up.

"Hello, sweetheart," she said.

"Hi, beautiful. Are you tucked in for the night?"

"Just about."

"I hope to see you soon. I'll let you know when I have a better idea of my travel plans. Good night, my angel."

"Good night, my darling."

The line was silent but alive with electricity transmitted between the two lovers.

Chapter 42

—•••—

HOT STEAMY AIR GREETED the travelers as they left the luxury cruise ship for a day of shopping in Port of La Guaira. The more adventurous souls climbed on the subway to explore the streets of Caracas. Most of them looked for a respite from the heat in the bars, restaurants, and shops on the waterfront.

Due to the extreme humidity, JJ's shirt stuck to his back wet with sweat. He entered Pablo's bar looking for relief from the heat as well as hoping to receive word about Pedro. He settled onto a chair at the far side of the bar away from most of the sweaty patrons. Starting to cool off under the lazy rotation of the fan overhead, he thought, *I could get to like this life. I could pull a Hemingway, no trouble at all.*

On his way to the bar, he had a call from Hutch pushing him to find Pedro. JJ was beginning to worry about the gardener. Why hadn't he returned from Baltimore, if that's where he spent the past week? Maybe he wasn't coming back. Yet, when JJ talked to him at his house just before he left, Pedro said he'd see him when he returned. JJ was furious with himself for losing Pedro at the airport.

His irritation rising, JJ walked outside the bar and stood looking out over the pier. He punched in Pedro's number more out of frustration than thinking he might find him at home. To his surprise, Pedro answered the phone.

"Pedro?" JJ asked, shocked. "Pedro, my man. I've been looking for you. This is JJ. We talked a few days ago, last week actually. You said you might be interested in a gardening job?"

"Ah, Señor JJ. Si, I remember. What property were you looking at again, por favor?"

"I'm considering the Sodano place. Coco gave me your name, remember?"

"Si, si, I remember. I'm very busy for the next two weeks with a project in downtown Caracas. But maybe after that we could talk," Pedro said.

"Pedro, I'm trying to decide if I should buy this piece of real estate. You know it very well, and it would be a big help to me if you could tell me if there is anything I need to watch out for. Could we meet there this afternoon so we could discuss the property? The sale is pending, but I don't want to go forward until I know how much it would cost to restore the gardens. I also want to know if you're interested in helping me when your project is completed."

"Ah, señor, it is time for my siesta. I am very tired. I just returned from a very stressful trip. But I suppose I could meet you at 6:30 this evening. It will still be light so we could look around. You can show me what you think should be done. Maybe you buy me dinner?"

"Pedro, 6:30 this evening will work for me. I'll meet you at the Sodana house."

JJ hung up and immediately called Hutch.

"Good news, partner. Pedro returned home. I'm meeting him this evening supposedly to discuss my potential purchase of a house and the conditions of the yard…no. Santiago hasn't returned to Caracas. The guys are on the lookout as you instructed."

—•••—

JJ MET Pedro at the house he purportedly was interested in buying. After wandering around the extensive garden of weeds and overgrown brush, JJ suggested they leave and discuss the job over dinner.

JJ couldn't believe how much the guy ate or how many beers he could tuck away at one meal. However, the two men came to an understanding on the scope of the job and how much Pedro would charge. JJ accepted the terms and told Pedro he would go ahead with the purchase. He would let Pedro know when the sale was completed so they could work out a schedule. Pedro thanked him for the dinner and left.

JJ met Pedro every night over the next seven days, buying him dinner and more beer. Not once did Pedro allude to any scheme he was working on in the States. Every night when he left JJ, Pedro always said he had another day of work on a project in Caracas. He thought the project would be finished in another couple of weeks at which time he could start on JJ's property, provided he owned it by then.

Of course, JJ and his team were watching Pedro every hour. He never left his house until he was ready to meet JJ at the end of the day for dinner. One hot afternoon, Pedro, working in his garden stripped off his shirt. The agent on watch took several pictures of Pedro's bare torso with his telephoto lens.

That night, when JJ returned to the base camp after dinner, the agent showed him the pictures he had taken that afternoon and had downloaded to the camp's computer. JJ quickly took the seat in front of the monitor and sent the pictures off to Hutch. As clear as day, Pedro had the same tattoo as John Anderson on his left arm just below the shoulder.

Chapter 43

— • • • —

NAVIGATING THE MOLLY C south to Ft. Lauderdale, Tony wished he had his dark glasses. Reflecting off the ocean, the sun shone bright and white-hot. He rummaged around in the drawers and other compartments hoping to find a pair. In a bottom drawer filled with tissues, notepads, and pens, he found a case containing polarized sunglasses. He quickly donned them and felt instant relief from the sun's glaring rays.

"How're you enjoying the ride so far, Mr. Bromley?" Tony asked when the man entered the cabin.

"Very smooth. You're doing a fine job. However, we're going to change course. The boat company that is going to take care of the Molly C is in Jacksonville, not Ft. Lauderdale. How long do you think it will take us to get to the Jacksonville area?"

"Well, I'll have to take a look at the chart, but I'm sure it will be several hours. We won't be able to make it before nightfall. We can drop anchor a little offshore along the way so we don't lose time docking," Tony said, reversing direction to head north.

"That'll be good," Bromley said. "I put provisions in the kitchen. Help yourself. You can have a snack now or wait for dinner. It's all the same. Some bananas, sandwiches and chips. Will you need help with the anchor?"

"No. I've been around boats all my life," Tony said congenially. "This baby's easy to handle. I'll let you know when we should stop for the night."

Bromley went back to his seat on the fantail. Tony text messaged Fred to let him know Bromley reversed course, and they now were headed to Jacksonville. He added he would text again when he dropped anchor for the night, and that he would try to find out their destination. He also added that all he had eaten were sandwiches and he looked forward to a couple of complimentary meals. He signed off with a smiley face.

Tony dropped anchor as the sun set and joined Bromley on the fantail.

"Can you show me on the map where we're headed?" Tony asked. "Then I can give you an estimate on how long it will take us to get there."

"Sure. We're going to pull in at the dock belonging to American Sails and Flags," Bromley said, pointing to a circled spot on the map he had laid on the small table.

The marine map gave Tony the coordinates for their destination. He estimated it would take an additional two hours from the time he lifted anchor in the morning. He gave this information to Bromley and then went below to a bunk located aft of the galley. Shortly after Tony went to bed, he heard Bromley heading to the forward stateroom.

— • • • —

IN THE STATEROOM, Bromley locked the door behind him. He stripped the bedding and mattress of the bed frame. Per Pedro's instructions, he opened the third compartment and found the metal box containing what he presumed was the ricin and removed it.

He remade the bed, leaving the spread on the floor. He was ready for a good night's sleep. But before turning in, he looked in the closet for a large windbreaker Pedro said Anderson put there. He tucked the box into the large inside pocket of the navy-blue jacket and then pulled out another set of clothes.

Should he need a quick disguise, he planned to layer what he wore in the morning. He added a few other pieces of clothing he thought would come in handy and stuffed the windbreaker into his duffel bag. Feeling prepared to disembark the Molly C once they arrived at the dock, Bromley went to bed and slept soundly.

— • • • —

TONY SCRUNCHED down under the bunk's covers and pulled out his cell. He sent a text to Fred that their destination was the dock of American Sails and Flags. He thought they would arrive between nine and eleven, depending on when Bromley got up in the morning. He ended the message asking for a tail to take over when they docked. He also asked for confirmation of his message.

Tony immediately received a text from Fred confirming the tail. Tony was to stay on him until the tail verbally relieved him. Tony closed his cell, pulled the sheet up and closed his eyes, but he didn't sleep. A lot depended on him tomorrow.

The next morning with the rising sun, Tony slipped into the galley and made a pot of coffee. He hoped the aroma would lure Bromley out of bed. Tony was anxious to wrap up his part of the caper. The rich aroma of coffee did the trick, and Bromley came out of the stateroom and poured himself a cup. Tony was checking out the map, which he had moved to the wheelhouse for navigation purposes. A little after ten o'clock, he pulled the Molly C alongside the dock of the sail company. Two maintenance men were waiting for him. Tony threw the lines out to them and positioned the fenders so the Molly C wouldn't scrape against the wooden structure.

"Well, Mr. Bromley, I guess we part company here."

"Yes, and thank you again for your help. Here's the hundred I promised you," Bromley said, placing a hundred dollar bill into Tony's hand. "You can ask the men on the dock how to get back to Daytona Beach."

Bromley seemed to be eager to get going, so both he and Tony left the Molly C at the same time. Tony hung back, ostensibly asking one of the maintenance men directions. He took note that Bromley went into a café located alongside the sail company.

Tony nonchalantly walked off the dock and entered the little café. He ordered a cup of coffee. Looking around he was surprised he didn't see Bromley. He was sure he didn't leave the building or Tony would have noticed him. He waited five minutes and then went to check the restroom. No one was there, but he saw stuffed in the trash barrel the sleeve of the shirt Bromley wore when he left the boat. Tony dashed out to the counter area. No Bromley. He looked in the kitchen. No sign of him. Tony went out the back entrance and ran into a large man.

"Your name Tony?" the man asked.

"Sure. Who are you?"

"I'm to relieve you of your tail. Where's the perp?"

"Shit. We've lost him." Rubbing his scalp in frustration, Tony muttered, *"I'm so fired."*

Chapter 44

— • • • —

SANTIAGO WAS BEING PRESSURED by his team for money. Now that the Molly C was in his possession at the sail company, the time had come to realize his gains from the drugs on board. His contact in Jacksonville was his favorite dealer—transactions swift and clean. He retrieved the man's number and punched in the code on his cell.

"Hello, Scottie. This is Luis. How are you?"

"Luis, my friend, everything is fine. Good to hear from you."

"How is your family? That boy of yours must be keeping you busy," Santiago said.

"Yes, he is. Let's see, it's been six months since you've seen him. He's in his terrible twos. At least that's what mothers call bad behavior here in Jacksonville."

"Scottie, I have a big sale for you. The bricks are the best and purest I've ever seen. They came straight from the lords in Venezuela."

"Sounds interesting, Luis. Where is this gold?"

"Practically under your nose, my dear friend. There is a boat tied up at the Sails and Flags dock. If I'm not mistaken, you can see her from your upstairs balcony."

"Luis, she *is* under my nose. Let me walk upstairs as we talk. Is the gold on this boat?"

"Yes. One of my operatives, a dock worker, is staying on her until the gold is removed, at which time he will sail away into the sunset."

"I'm on my balcony, Luis. Is the boat of which you speak about thirty-feet long?"

"No no no. She is forty-four feet of pure beauty. Do you see her?" Santiago asked.

"Yes, I do see her. She is tied up at the north end of their pier. How many bricks are we talking about, Luis?"

"One-hundred-eight bricks in total. One kilo each.

"I say, that *would* be a big sale. How much are you asking for me to take this stuff off your hands?"

"You are aware that I know what the street value of such pure gold is worth," Santiago countered. "You should be able to get $26,000 for each brick when you break it down into small packets. We can both do the math."

"Oh, my dear friend, there is no way I could get such money. You are talking in the neighborhood of almost three-million dollars for the load. This leaves me no profit and I must take all the risk and do all the work."

"Scottie, I'm aware of what you say. Because I need capital for an operation in no less than seven days, I will give it to you for half price. What do you say? Can you turn it over in seven days?"

"Luis, I could pick up the stuff in ten days but not before. I'm what you might say *hot* right now. I dare not make a move before then. I give you twenty-five percent of the one million when the bricks are removed from your boat. The balance will take me four or five days. My distributors pay promptly unless, of course, I can't find them," Scottie said, chuckling.

"Scottie, this is no laughing matter. I require one-and-one-half million in seven days or I go somewhere else."

"Luis, my friend, where else are you going to go? The boat, she is here. The gold, she is here. I am here. And, you, Luis, need the capital for your operation in a hurry. No one will give you a better deal and you know it."

"You drive a hard bargain, Scottie. Call my cell number as soon as you can begin the deal. Don't go aboard the Molly C without calling me first, or you will end up with a hole in your heart. My man has orders to shoot to kill if anyone tries to board."

"The Molly C? Seems like I've heard that name recently," Scottie mused.

Chapter 45

— • • • —

CATHERINE STOOD UP from her design table and stretched. Her back ached, her head ached, and her fingers were stiff. A hot bubble bath would be just the answer to relieve all the aches and pains. With a glass of wine, she immersed herself into the bubbles and thought about Hutch. He was now the love of her life. Thoughts of him lingered after her bath, through dinner, and then into her dreams.

The next morning she rose early completely refreshed. Her first stop was an early meeting with Russell Stone to show him her design for the marina restaurant.

After looking at her work, Russell said he liked the drawings and only made a few structural suggestions. While at Stone & Associates, Catherine received a call from the frame shop. The certifications for the auction's two honorees were ready to be picked up. Daytona Pete and Peaches were such big hits that she had created official awards for them, in addition to the plaques they were given at the event.

Catherine swung by the shop and picked up the framed work on her way home. The rest of the day she spent in her design studio adapting Russell's suggestions. At 4:30 that afternoon, standing and rubbing her back, stiff again from bending over the blueprints all day, she decided to give Manny a call to see if she could drop off Peaches' certification. She called the department, and Manny said he would be delighted to meet with her, but rather than coming into town, he suggested meeting him at his houseboat in an hour. He threw in an offer for a glass of wine, which sealed the bargain.

"This will give me a much needed break today. I'll take a hot shower and let the water beat on my back," she said to herself, rubbing the achy lower muscles.

An hour later she parked in Manny's driveway. I'll never get tired of this beautiful scene—his houseboat tied to the dock with all the forested land bordering the river. *It must be a wonderful retreat for someone who sees the ugly side of life every day,* she thought.

Peaches made a flying leap off the boat and raced up the driveway, immediately sitting in front of her and waiting for her greeting. Peaches was not disappointed. Catherine juggled the framed certificate, and her bag, and gave Peaches a loving scratch behind each ear all the while cooing the beauty of the dog.

Manny stepped out on the fantail of his houseboat and gave her a wave. She walked down the driveway to meet him.

"Hello, Captain," she said, greeting him with a quick peck on his check.

"What have you been up to, Cat, since I last saw you, which I guess was the auction?" Manny asked. "First, however, let's go down to the galley so I can pour that glass of wine I promised you and then I want to hear everything." *Oh, she smells so sweet,* he thought.

"That sounds wonderful. I was bent over blueprints most of the day. When I called you, I could barely stand up. I have a big job which is turning out to be all consuming, at Pelican Bay Marina. I had a meeting with Russell today, and he gave me some architectural changes."

Manny handed her a glass of wine and poured a glass of scotch for himself.

"Cheers to you, my friend," she said. "May you keep capturing all the bad guys."

"I'll certainly drink to that," Manny said, as they touched glass to glass.

"No wine for you?" she asked, noting the stiff drink in his hand.

"Well, at the end of the day I find something a little stronger helps to relieve the tensions from the past twenty-four hours. Would you care for some scotch?"

"No, this wine is just right," Catherine said, sliding onto the bench and picked up a picture lying on the galley table.

"Manny, this is an interesting design shown in this photo. I've seen this graphic before, but I can't think where."

"You have? It's a tattoo graphic."

"Manny, are you going hippie on me? Wait a minute. I know where I saw it."

"Where was that?" Manny said, leaning forward over the table.

"At the marina. Yes. It was the first meeting I had with Ted Adams. He approached me at the auction about doing some work at the marina. I met with him the following Monday. Anyway, at the end of the meeting he was walking me to the front entrance, but there was something going on outside, something unpleasant down on his dock. He excused himself and ran down to help. I don't know what the commotion was about, but he stripped his shirt off before getting into the water by the boat that was tied up. Yes, that's when I saw it. Ted has a tattoo just like this."

"Are you sure, Cat? This is just something that Dani picked out of a book. She's into tattoos and stuff like this," Manny said, finishing off his drink.

"I'm quite sure. I passed the side entrance as I was leaving and saw the altercation. Ted wasn't far away from me because the dock is just a few steps down from where I stood. I saw this tattoo clearly. Rather like a condor, don't you think?"

Chapter 46

—•••—

HUTCH'S CELL BEEPED at him as he entered his townhouse. Juggling a large bag of Chinese takeout from down the street, he pulled the phone off his belt. The cell displayed a conference call connection. Hutch put the phone on the counter and turned up the volume as he deposited the bag on the kitchen table.

"What's up, guys? Is this going to be a short conversation or a long one, so I can dig out my pork-fried rice as we talk," he chuckled, retrieving a plate from the cupboard.

"I, on the other hand have a steaming hot bowl of Jambalaya, made special for me by Agnes, my housekeeper," Pete countered.

"If you two guys would stop thinking about your stomachs and listen to me," Manny barked.

"Okay, don't get testy," Pete said.

"Catherine stopped by just now to drop off a framed certificate for Peaches. We were having a drink in the galley when she asked me about a photo that was lying on the table. She said she'd seen the design before but couldn't remember where."

"What was the subject of the photo?" Hutch asked. *Geez, why was she having drinks with Manny?*

"It was a print of the photo taken of Anderson's tattoo," Manny said.

"Did she remember where she saw it?" Hutch asked, the pork fried rice now forgotten.

"Yes—"

"Where?" Hutch barked.

"When I told her it was a photo of a tattoo, she immediately remembered. She had an afternoon meeting with Ted Adams the Monday after the auction. When she was leaving the marina there was a commotion on the dock. Adams charged down to help. He took his shirt off, and she saw the tattoo on his arm."

"Holy shit," Pete exclaimed.

"And Ted sold the boat before you asked him to," Hutch said. "Have you heard from your guy Tony again? Where did they moor? The buyer's name was Charles Bromley? Anything on him?" Hutch demanded.

"Wait just a minute, Agent Hutchinson. Catherine just left and I called you immediately. I suggest *you* check out this Charles Bromley. I'll see if we've had any more communication with Tony. I propose we both see what we can learn about Ted Adams. What I do know about him is that he's been the general manager of the marina for around three years, but I have to verify that. Dani learned that he served in the Air Force."

"Okay, Manny," Hutch said. "Add Adams to your surveillance detail. I'll get an agent down to take over in case he leaves Florida. See if you can find out where he was the day of the Preakness."

Chapter 47

— • • • —

TED ADAMS WAS BUSY at his desk cranking in numbers on his spreadsheet. With his take from Santiago, the renovation of the marina was in the bag. The principal partners offered him a full partnership in the operation with the $500,000 he said he would invest. They stepped up with additional funds and gave him the green light to go ahead with the expansion.

Adams reminisced about his tour of duty in the Air Force, which was bitter sweet. He enjoyed the technical aspects of keeping the planes in perfect order, but he hated the regime of the military. He continually bucked his superiors and barely escaped a dishonorable discharge.

When he mustered out, he moved as far away from his last deployment as he could get. Within a couple of years he had talked his way into managing Pelican Bay Marina.

Santiago selected him for the condor mission because he was an aeronautical engineer. He attended the University of Washington and worked his way through school at the Seattle Yacht Club. His love of the water, and the experience of tending to the beautiful boats at the club, sealed the desire to own a marina.

When at the suggestion of John Anderson, Santiago recruited him, he wasn't too sure he wanted to be involved. But the more Santiago and Anderson talked about their scheme the more excited he became. He needed a lot of money and Santiago's offer appeared to be the only way he was ever going to get it.

His part of the operation was a challenge. As an aeronautical engineer, he felt sure that he could build the drone. He'd actually built a few during his short time in the Air Force. Programming and guiding the drone with a GPS was not difficult either. Remotely detonating the small explosive device at the exact time to release the ricin mist was a little trickier, but after several experiments with the timer as a backup, the device worked perfectly. The test in Baltimore proved that all his mechanical and engineering efforts were indeed accurate. He knew he could deliver his part of the bargain.

Ted hit the save button and closed the file. Taking a break from his work, he went out to the bar for a fresh cup of coffee. He stood in front of the window sipping his coffee, enjoying the view of the river. Only a few more days and he would be a partner. Topping off his cup, he returned to his office, closed the door, locking it securely behind him.

When he met the others in Baltimore, he took spare parts with him—backup GPS, remotes, and an explosive device. He also took extra parts for the drone itself, in case it was damaged en route to Belmont, New York.

Again he went to his computer and opened a hidden file, Triple Crown. After checking the list of equipment he needed for Santiago, he saved and closed the document. The drone was ready to fly again. Like a boomerang, she had circled back after flying over Pimlico. The small, pilotless plane landed in the street in front of the warehouse as soft as a breath of air. The team carefully packed the condor in the rented POD, and Santiago delivered the container safely to the warehouse in Belmont.

Sitting back in his chair, a smile crossed Adams' face. Just a few more days and my dream of owning a high-class marina in a prestigious community will come true, he thought. I'll be one of the most successful businessmen on the east coast of Florida. He packed up his laptop computer, retrieved a suitcase from the closet, and left for the airport.

Chapter 48

—•••—

CATHERINE PACKED HER BRIEFCASE as carefully as she did her overnight bag. The structural blueprints for the marina expansion were finished, pending any changes the builder might suggest. She was now to the point where furniture ideas needed to be gathered to show Ted Adams. She was also on the lookout for tables and chairs for the cyber café.

Hutch said he was going to be traveling until after the weekend so his absence afforded her the opportunity to go to New York City's furniture district. Most of the furniture establishments catered only to professional decorators. The public was not allowed unless accompanied by their designer. Her direct flight from Orlando to LaGuardia, NYC, took just a little over two hours.

Catherine was on the road to Orlando International Airport by six in the morning. The database on her laptop gave her quick access to all the salespeople she wanted to see. She had plenty of time in the air to map out her stops once she arrived in the furniture district.

The flight was scheduled to depart on time and she cleared security quickly. A veteran traveler, she wore no belt, her shoes slipped off easily, and all fluids were in no more than three-ounce containers. She arrived at the gate forty minutes before boarding time and settled in a chair for the wait.

"Oh no," she said to herself.

The woman next to her looked up, "What did you say, dear?"

"I just remembered something. Can you watch my bag for a second? I'll be over by that window. I have to make a phone call," She replied.

"Of course, but do stay by the window. You know what they say about watching someone else's bag," the woman replied.

Catherine quickly found Hutch's number stored on her phone and punched Send. His voicemail kicked in. *He must be in a meeting and has his cell turned off,* she thought.

"Hi, sweetheart. I'm at the Orlando airport," she said. "I'll be boarding a flight to New York in a few minutes. I'm just staying overnight, back tomorrow. I'm very excited because I'll be visiting the furniture district to pick out possibilities for the marina and connecting with some of my friends. Hope you have a wonderful day. Kisses."

I'm not going to call Manny, she thought. *I'll be back tomorrow, no need to bother him.* She took her seat in the waiting area and thanked the woman next to her for watching her bag. Within twenty minutes, she was on the plane, strapped in, and ready for her New York field trip. The flight was smooth and uneventful. She barely finished her coffee and mapping out her itinerary for her stay in the city when the pilot notified the passengers to stow their tray tables and put their seat backs in their upright position.

Catherine took a cab from the airport to the first outlet on her list. Entering the building just before noon, she showed the security attendant her architect's license and signed the registry logbook. Familiar with the layout of the galleries, she went to the section displaying tables, chairs, and breakfronts for restaurants. She also looked at dining-room suites for the home. Sometimes she found designs she liked better in the home galleries.

The day passed quickly, too quickly. She visited only three of the seven furniture establishments on her list. She gave Tillie a quick call to let her know she had seen some possibilities for the café but nothing said, "buy me," yet. It was almost five in the afternoon when she bumped into a friend, Patty Clark, whom she went to school with at the Rhode Island School of Design. The two women hugged and Patty insisted on taking Catherine to dinner.

"There is a little Italian place around the corner that is to die for," Patty said. "Besides, then we can catch up."

Catherine fell into bed by nine-thirty, thoroughly exhausted but excited about the items she'd seen. Tomorrow was going to be another big day. Her return flight left LaGuardia at eight in the evening, so she had to make the most of her time.

At ten o'clock the next morning, Catherine hit pay dirt. She found just what she was looking for, and the salesman was going to give her a great deal because of the large number of tables and chairs she said her client would require. Digging her cell out of her bag, she put a call through to Ted Adams. The receptionist at the marina said he was out, but Catherine could reach him on his cell. The woman gave Catherine the number and she called him immediately.

"Hi, Ted, it's Catherine. I think I've found just the furniture to make your new restaurant the showplace of Daytona Beach. I'm in New York at Bernadini's Furniture Emporium. I'll take some pictures and send them to you. If you like what you see, maybe you could take a trip here in the next couple of weeks—"

"What, you're in New York now?" Catherine asked. "Yes, I'll wait for you, and lunch sounds perfect. Ask the cab to take you to Bernadini's in the furniture district. It's huge. If you have any problem, call me back on my cell. You have the number, I think. ...good."

Catherine closed her phone, deposited it into her bag and went to look for the salesman she'd been dealing with. *What a lucky day this is turning out to be,* she thought.

—•••—

AT THE WAREHOUSE a few miles from Belmont Park Race Track, Ted told Santiago he was going to have lunch with his architect. He didn't have anything left to contribute to the operation until that night. His piece of the plan was ready to go, so he might as well do something useful.

Ted took a cab into the city. The driver dropped him off in front of the furniture outlet. Catherine was waiting for him at the door so she could sign him in as her guest. He followed her to the gallery where she'd seen the furniture. After looking at her suggestions, he had to agree that the pieces would make his dining room spectacular. She introduced him to the salesman, and they made arrangements for Ted to call within two weeks to finalize the deal. The extra days would give Catherine the time she needed to lay everything out to scale, so the order would be accurate.

"I don't have a clue as to where to go to lunch in this area of the city," Ted said.

"Last night my friend introduced me to this fabulous little Italian restaurant. It's only a couple of blocks from here. Are you game?" she asked.

Ted nodded in agreement and after a fifteen-minute walk they were seated at a table off to the side but near the window. They discussed the furniture and the possible layout of the room. He calculated the number of tables and chairs the space would require. Allowing for two seatings, he figured how many patrons he could accommodate in an evening, or a busy lunch hour, to enable him to reach his income goal for the dining room.

Ted ordered a fine Merlot to accompany their pasta salad. Their conversation turned to chit chat about Catherine's various design jobs.

"You'll never guess what I saw the other day," Catherine said. "I was visiting Manny Salinas, you know Captain Salinas?"

"Yes, I know him quite well," Ted said. "I stored the beached boat at the marina, the one where they found the dead man."

Ted's reminder of the dead man made Catherine wish she'd been able to fulfill her promise to Hutch. She was supposed to let him know if she was going to a meeting at the marina, or if she was planning to leave town. *Oh well,* she thought, *I did leave him a message, and I'll be home in a few hours.*

"As I was saying, I went to Manny's houseboat to give him Peaches' framed certificate from the auction when she was honored. On his kitchen table was a picture of your tattoo."

"What tattoo?" Ted asked, putting his glass down, sitting up ramrod straight in his chair.

"The one on your arm. I noticed it at our first meeting. You ran down to the dock just below the side entrance to help your men. When you took your shirt off, I noticed your tattoo. It's quite unusual. Almost a caricature of a condor. Anyway, I told Manny that I had seen that graphic on your shoulder. He said it must be popular because his tech was thinking of getting one just like it."

"Really? Well, that is interesting," Ted said, scanning the room, looking out the window making a visual sweep of the street. "Where are you heading now, Catherine?"

"Because I was so lucky in finding furniture samples you like, I guess back to the airport. Maybe I can get an earlier return flight.

When I checked out this morning, I brought my overnight case with me so I wouldn't have to go back to the hotel."

"How about I drop you off at the airport on my way back to my meeting? I'm visiting a warehouse to see different types of boat-storage lifts. I need better equipment that's adaptable to various sized boats I pull them out of the water for storage."

"Well, if it's not out of your way, I'll take you up on your offer."

"Tell you what, Catherine, if you have an extra hour, I'd like your opinion, from an architectural point-of-view, on the storage scheme this company offers. Could you spare the time, and then I'll get you to the airport?"

"I guess that's the least I can do after you bought my lunch," she said smiling.

Ted hailed a cab and gave the driver an address written on a piece of paper. Ted closed the door of the cab and went around to the trunk to put his briefcase inside. With the trunk lid open, he made a call on his cell.

"Luis, we have a big problem," he said softly. "I'm bringing a little insurance with me, a woman. Prepare the office for her. You know the drill." Ted cut the connection and joined Catherine in the cab.

Chapter 49

—•••—

THE RIDE WAS PLEASANT from downtown New York City to the tree-lined streets of Belmont. The cab driver pulled up to the address he was given and stopped in front of a gate. The property was enclosed by a chain-link fence within which Catherine could see a very large warehouse.

Three cars were inside the fence, parked to the right of what appeared to be a front entrance. There was no sign on the fence or on the warehouse indicating the name of the company. Ted paid the cab and opened the car door for Catherine. The cab driver retrieved her overnight bag and Ted's briefcase from the trunk and then pulled away down the street.

"I have a car parked inside the gate," Ted said, "so I'll be able to get you to the airport after you've seen the equipment." Ted flipped open his cell and punched in a number.

"Hello, Luis. Miss Hainsworth and I are out front. Will you buzz the gate for us? ...thank you."

Ted and Catherine passed through the gate, which swung closed behind them. They continued down the cement walkway toward the front door.

"Whoever owns this property certainly doesn't take very good care of it," Catherine said. "Just look at the debris."

"I know, but at least their equipment is some of the best I've seen."

When they reached the front entrance, Ted moved in front of Catherine, pushing the door open for her to enter. As she did so, a man with a ski mask grabbed her. He shoved her hard into an old office causing her to lose her balance. As she was falling, Ted yelled out indicating he, too, was under attack but being pushed in a different direction. The door slammed shut behind Catherine. Suddenly, everything fell silent.

Inside the warehouse to the right of a large open area were three long folding tables and four chairs. The two men, who had so roughly greeted Catherine and Ted, walked over and sat down. Ted joined them. He picked up a bottle of water, unscrewed the cap, and took a long swallow.

"Do you mind telling me what this is all about?" Santiago asked angrily.

"I think the law may be on to us. Miss Hainsworth is friendly with the captain at the Daytona Police Department. She evidently saw my tattoo when she visited the marina. She told me she saw an identical photo in the captain's possession. I could be wrong, but they may think the tattoo on Anderson could be linked to his killer, or to a group," Ted said.

Ted paused, taking another long swallow of water.

"We don't know if they found the bricks." Ted continued. "Let's say they did discover the stuff. They're then looking for more than a killer. They'd look for smugglers, smugglers as in more than one. If she told the cops I had a tattoo, then I've been burned. After the mission, if there's no trouble, you can pretend to free us. However, if the law is onto us, we'll have a bargaining chip. Remember, if they know about the stuff, they think a man named Charles Bromley bought the Molly C. Bromley doesn't exist. Have you heard anything more from Brownhill?"

"Yes. Christopher called an hour ago," Santiago said. "He gave me good news and some bad news. The good news is he has prepared the castor beans Pedro brought to our meeting in Baltimore, when we tested the drone at the Preakness. In his home laboratory, he packaged the ricin in the delivery device. He plans to join us tomorrow morning no later than ten o'clock. He has an early morning flight from Rutland, Vermont, to Manchester, New Hampshire, and then to New York."

"What's the bad news?" Pedro asked.

"The container Brownhill retrieved from the Molly C, the one you had filled with ricin in Port of La Guaira, was filled with flour. Somehow the original stash was removed from the Molly C. So, my friends, we have come to a 'Y' in the road. Do we go forward tomorrow? Or, do we abort right now?"

"I vote we go ahead, damn imperialists. I want them to feel the fear they spread around the world," Pedro said, throwing the empty bottle of water against the wall. Not the usual plastic container, the glass bottle shattered.

"Well, my friends, have either of you felt you were being watched? Have you had any indications you were followed?"

"Santiago, please. With the rules you put in place when we move about to meet together, how could anybody follow us?" Pedro said. "I've pulled many disappearing acts at the Caracas airport."

"Catherine seeing a tattoo like mine could be chalked up to coincidence," Ted said. "I haven't seen or felt anyone following me. I say let's continue. Besides, once we launch the drone everything is on automatic, so we can clear out of here, no one the wiser. You two and Brownhill can leave first. Then I'll let Hainsworth out, complaining how we were both attacked, and that the company and equipment I was bringing her to see must have been a fraud."

"It would be a shame to abort such a perfect scheme," Santiago said, looking over at the drone gleaming in the dim light of the warehouse. "We don't have to venture out of this building until the beauty is launched. We open the garage door, we launch her, we close the door, and we go home. We drive away from the wind, if there is one, so we have no chance of exposing ourselves to the toxin."

"The test at the Preakness proved the preprogrammed GPS is working perfectly," Adams said. "The timing device dropped the banner at the exact time I set. One button, just one button to send the bird on its way, is all we have to push. Hell, it only has to fly two miles, and it's over the race track."

"When I talked to Brownhill," Santiago said, "he was for going ahead with the mission. So, my friends, I guess it is unanimous. Tomorrow we will enter the history books."

Chapter 50

—•••—

DOWN THE ROAD, a scant half mile from the warehouse, sat a three-bay, abandoned automobile repair shop. Its cement block walls were covered with vines with the exception of a boarded-up front window. Weed infested gravel surrounded the building, but the property was not enclosed with a fence.

Beginning at two in the afternoon, three dirty white vans pulled around the back at half-hour intervals. A garage door lifted to let a van in, and then closed after the vehicle entered the building. After each van parked, it disgorged members of Hutch's SWAT team. They systematically lined up their gear including hazmat suits. In a dimly lit room in the back of the building, the men congregated, waiting for their instructions. The last van was swallowed into the building allowing the men inside to clamor off, stash their gear, and join their teammates.

Hutch put a call into Manny. He wanted Tony Sullivan to join the team as soon as possible. Tony was the only one who had seen the fourth terrorist. A government plane would meet Tony at the Daytona Beach Airport in an hour to fly him to New York. He would be met by an agent who would escort him to the command center for Operation Big Brown.

After his call to Manny, Hutch took the floor to layout the mission to his team.

"So far each of you has been read into the severity of the situation. A potential terrorist attack by a drone outfitted with a spray tank, or tanks, that by remote control or timer could deliver a biological agent. We believe this particular group is unaffiliated to any known terrorists. The group appears to be held together by a hatred of the United States. To our knowledge, they have not identified their group with a name, but each of the four members has a tattoo of a condor, a bird of prey, on his left arm just below the shoulder." Hutch paused to tape a picture of the tattoo to the grimy cement wall of the room.

"We believe this group is comprised of four members. Luis Santiago, a former jockey and now race handicapper, seems to be the leader," Hutch said, again pausing to tape Santiago's picture to the wall next to the tattoo.

"Pedro Riveras, gardener. We believe he delivered the castor beans necessary to make the biological substance ricin. Ted Adams, an aeronautical engineer, who we think put together the drone, the navigation system, and remote control equipment."

At the introduction of each man, Hutch taped his picture to the wall.

"The fourth member of the group is Charles Bromley. Unfortunately, we haven't been able to locate this man. We don't know anything about him, but our guess is he has the expertise to refine the castor beans into an aerosol powder. Here's his picture. As you can see, he has the tattoo on his left arm." Hutch taped Bromley's picture beside the rest of the gallery.

"Santiago, Riveras, and Bromley have outsmarted us at almost every turn. Several times we've had them tailed successfully only to lose them. The only man we tailed successfully is Ted Adams. He led us to the warehouse down the road, from where we are confident they are going to try to launch their attack. Santiago and Riveras have been seen entering the building. The fourth man has not arrived, and because of him we cannot launch our raid. We must be sure we get all the players, the drone, and the paraphernalia required for their attack. They must not be allowed to escape and come back to hit us another day."

Hutch again tried to swallow a little bit of the cold water.

"There are four agents positioned in the woods around the warehouse. They are our eyeballs for any activity outside the building. However, there is an extenuating circumstance. Isn't there always?" he said, looking at the men gathered around him. "About two hours ago, one of the agents radioed me that a cab pulled up to the gate. Ted Adams stepped out of the cab with a woman. The cab left, the gate swung open, and he and the woman entered the compound. The gate swung closed behind them. When they got to the door, Adams pushed the door open. The lady stepped in. The agent couldn't see her once she entered the doorway, but he thought he heard a muffled scream. He was pretty sure that's what he heard, but it could have been an animal in the woods behind him."

"So who is the lady?" a team member asked.

"I'm getting to that," Hutch said. "Because of the tail we had on Adams, we know he met this woman for lunch, and that they both got into the cab. Our man tailed the cab to the warehouse. We know who the woman is. Her name is Catherine Hainsworth, an architect from Daytona Beach. We do not believe, let me put it stronger, we *know* she has nothing to do with the group and was taken as a hostage."

It was all Hutch could do to keep his hand from shaking as he taped Catherine's picture with the others on the dirty wall.

Hutch passed out bottles of water to his team. He opened a bottle and tried to swallow, but the thought of Catherine in danger caused the liquid to stick in his throat.

"Because the horse Big Brown won the Kentucky Derby and the Preakness, he is eligible to take the honor of winning the Triple Crown," Hutch said. "Big Brown is favored to win the race and millions of people will tune in worldwide to see it. In fact, the horse could pull off racing history."

"I've watched the Belmont Stakes in the past, and you're right, it attracts people from many countries," a SWAT member added.

"The race is scheduled to run at 6:30 tomorrow evening," Hutch continued. "Because it's our theory that the terrorists will want the biggest audience possible for their dirty deed, we don't think they'll launch the drone prior to that time. But we can't be sure. We have an officer in route who will join our guys surveilling the warehouse. He's the only person who has actually seen the fourth man. We have his picture, but to be extra careful, Tony Sullivan will be taking up the watch with the others in about three hours. Our agents monitoring the warehouse will alert us when the fourth man arrives. If for some reason he doesn't show, we'll get in position forty minutes prior to the running of the race."

Again Hutch tried to swallow some water. He choked, spitting out what remained in his mouth. "I've obtained plans for the warehouse including electrical work. At eighteen hundred hours, one member of our SWAT team will disable the warning system on the fence and the gate. Two others will cut holes in the fence to give us access in front of the bay doors as well as the opposite side of the building and in back."

"When do we form the teams?" a big guy asked—leaning forward, itching to get started.

"Tomorrow. I'll break you up into three groups. You'll enter the compound from one of the three openings cut in the fence. Two teams will swarm in when the bay door lifts. The third team will enter through the front door."

"What about the lady?" a team member asked.

"We don't know where the hostage will be, but according to these plans, there is an office with a bathroom immediately to the left of the front door. She may be in there. I believe the four terrorists will be in the warehouse, licking their chops as they wait for the moment the drone takes off, which, gentlemen, *must not happen!* Lives of thousands of innocent spectators depend on us stopping the drone. Any questions?"

"Ok, can't we just go in now and smash the bastards?" asked another member of the SWAT team.

"As I said, we have to wait for the fourth man," Hutch explained. "Without him, they may not even have the ricin in their possession. So we would net three guys having fun with a toy airplane and perhaps abusing a woman. Now, I suggest you all get something to eat. There are plenty of MREs in the vans, also air mattresses for tonight. You can use flashlights because the windows are boarded on the outside and blackout sheets cover the inside. We'll go over final instructions tomorrow morning."

—•••—

IT WAS CLOSE to midnight and still no activity at the warehouse was reported by his surveillance team. Hutch sat down on his mattress in the back room, head down, worried sick about Catherine. The light on his cell phone blinked with an incoming call. It was Catherine.

"Catherine, are you all right? ...yes, I know where you are. Did they hurt you? ...a scraped knee? Remind me to kiss it better when I see you tomorrow...yes, tomorrow...a man pushed you in a room to the left of the front door? Catherine, listen carefully to me. When we disconnect, hide the phone somewhere in the room. You don't want them to find it on you, or they may suspect you called for help."

Hutch tried to keep his emotions in check. His mind quickly accepting, discarding, accepting a new idea on how Catherine could help herself in this dangerous position.

"Second, you're stuck where you are until late in the day tomorrow. If at any time you hear a commotion, get as far away as you can from the inside walls and particularly the door to the room you're in. There may be gunfire, and I want you in a corner on the floor until I or one of my men comes to get you. Got that? Be brave, my darling. I promise it won't be long. Catherine, please remember I love you with all my heart."

Chapter 51

—•••—

ALL DAY PETE TRIED to get into his groove to prepare for tomorrow's race for the Triple Crown. The more he tried to gather the statistics on the horses in the race, the more frustrated he became. His thoughts kept reverting to Hutch's operation to take down the terrorists. Regardless, he was making headway in spite of himself. Santiago's blog handicapped the race the same in the morning as late in the day. Pete would check again tomorrow morning for any last minute upgrades to the information.

He was going all out, putting everything he had won in the Preakness on the line. He thought Big Brown would win, even though he had a crack in his hoof. The owner, trainer, and veterinarian said he was good to go. However, betting on a sure thing had burned him more than once, so he hedged his bets, always putting two or three other horses in each position along with Big Brown. Pete was definitely going to bet all the exotic types of wagers—the exacta, trifecta, and superfecta.

At midnight his nerves were still wired, but he knew tomorrow was going to be a big, long, and very dangerous day. He should try to get some sleep. He took off the cap of his favorite beer and rolled out to his balcony to enjoy the starry night. Settled into his wheelchair and listening to the ebb and flow of the gentle waves on the shore below, he was interrupted by the ringing of his cell. He unclipped his phone and saw it was Hutch.

"Hey, you shithead, how's it going up north?" Pete asked. "What? …they have Catherine? How in the name of God did that happen? …I see. Well, that sure complicates things doesn't it? …No, nothing in the blog today. Is Santiago in that warehouse? ...Excellent. Well, good luck, buddy. I'll be praying for you ...and Catherine. If I see anything or have any new information to give you, I'll call. Take care, buddy. Bye."

Chapter 52

—•••—

Belmont Stakes, race for the Triple Crown

THE CONDOR GROUP didn't sleep. Finally, at six o'clock in the morning, Santiago couldn't lie still another minute. Rising from his pallet on the floor, he went over to the makeshift kitchen and started the coffee. Ted and Pedro joined him. The three men sat at the table in silence.

Santiago broke the spell to go over all the plans for the day, hopeful that he hadn't missed anything.

"My friends, we have waited for this day, and I trust all our dreams will be accomplished," Santiago said. "As a precaution, in the event they are on to us, I purchased some firearms—a Glock 9mm with two extra clips for each of you and Christopher when he arrives. They are in the box next to the food supplies. Pedro, bring a gun to me and one for Ted if you please. Arm yourself as well. I'm pleased to say, we have no indication we are under suspicion. We just sit now and wait for Christopher."

Santiago sat back in the chair, confident the day would proceed according to plan. He glanced over at the sleek, silver drone sitting serenely on the cement floor just sixty feet from the huge bay door. He visualized the bird gathering speed as the door lifted, allowing her to flee the cage and fly to her destination.

Santiago, unaware that overnight a storm slammed into New England out of the Great Lakes and Buffalo, flipped open his ringing cell.

"Christopher, this better be important to break the blackout. ...a storm? Your flight is delayed? Is there any chance you won't be here on time? It looks like three o'clock for sure? Christopher, the weather here is beautiful. If you see any problem with your new timetable, call immediately."

Santiago, slammed his cell shut, jamming it into his pocket.

—•••—

HUTCH CALLED JJ, who was in charge of the warehouse stakeout. "No Bromley yet, I take it?" he asked.

"Nope, but Tony Sullivan arrived and is on the lookout. Maybe Bromley's not part of the group."

"My gut says he is. With him or without him, we start the operation at three o'clock. My team will join your surveillance. Their hazmat gear is rolled up in a backpack. They will walk through the woods in groups of three. I'll bring up the rear and join you on the garage side of the building."

At three o'clock, Hutch's team started their journey to the warehouse. As planned, they each joined one of the three groups. Per their instructions, and on command, the first task was to cut a hole in the fence for their group to enter the compound.

The minutes crawled by. Still no sight of a fourth man. Hutch checked his watch. It was now 5:20; five minutes had passed since he last checked. His training was now in command of his body—breathing slowed, nerves calm, eyes constantly scanning the target area.

A cab slowed and stopped at the gate. A man emerged—his head in the car as he paid the fare. He stepped away from the cab.

Six agents plus ten SWAT members heard at once over their earpieces. "It's Bromley. The fourth man has arrived. It's twenty-five minutes to race time," Hutch whispered.

Christopher Brownhill, otherwise known as Charles Bromley, watched the cab drive out of sight, then dug out his cell phone. A minute later, the front door of the warehouse opened, and Santiago walked briskly to the gate to let Brownhill through. The two men hugged briefly and ran back inside the warehouse, closing the door behind them.

Hutch radioed Team C on the other side of the warehouse to breach the fence and cut the alarm system. The leader of Team C radioed back shortly that the alarm had been disabled. Hutch radioed all leaders to commence with the operation.

Holes were cut in the fence and quietly sixteen agents surrounded the compound. Two groups lined up on each side of the garage entrance, ready to rush it when the big door opened. The third group quickly positioned itself on either side of the front entrance.

The only sound outside was the shrill squawk of a vulture. All eyes were trained on their respective targets. The low groan of the huge garage door mechanism was heard and grew louder as the heavy door rose. About a foot off the ground, the engine of the drone meshed with the noise of the door. At three feet off the ground, words of instruction were heard over the din of the rising door and the drone's engine. At four feet, the agents rushed the building.

Someone pushed the remote control button of the drone because it started to inch forward. The bay door had reached its apex when gunfire broke out. Hutch saw that the drone was gaining speed. He raced to the button to send the heavy bay door back down its tracks.

The door was within three feet of being closed when the drone approached, picking up speed as it began its ascent. But it wasn't fast enough to escape to freedom. At full power, the silver bird slammed into the closing warehouse door. The drone fell to the ground, broken like a bird in flight crashing into a window.

Hutch turned away from the door just as Santiago was thrown to the ground repeatedly firing his gun. His aim was on the mark hitting Hutch in the side of his arm. The bullet traveled into his body, and another bullet hit him in the thigh. Hutch crumpled to the floor. JJ radioed the white van equipped with medical equipment for assistance, yelling at them to hurry. An agent was down. The medical team entered the front door of the warehouse in seconds. Rushing to Hutch's side, they lifted him onto the stretcher, raced back to the van, and took off at high speed.

The stretcher carrying Hutch passed Tony Sullivan as he was breaking down the door to the room where Catherine was thought to be. He quickly stepped through the broken door. She was huddled in the corner, afraid to move.

"Catherine, I'm with Hutch's team. You're safe now," he said, rushing to her.

"Where's Hutch?" she asked, eyes frightened. She slowly rose to her feet with Tony's help.

Not answering her, Tony said, "Stay here a minute. I have to be sure it's safe to leave the room."

The scene in the warehouse was organized chaos as they yelled to one another. Three agents, suited up in hazmat gear, were removing a cylinder from the belly of the broken drone.

White sheets covered three bodies. Santiago, crying out in pain, was being removed on a stretcher. His knee appeared to be shattered—a tourniquet wound around his thigh.

"Who's down?" Tony called out to a SWAT member rushing by him.

"Charles Bromley, who I've been told is really Christopher Brownhill. He was the fourth man. Pedro Riveras and Ted Adams are also dead. No agents are down except for Hutchinson. JJ, the agent who raced out with Hutch on the stretcher, radioed back that he was lost to us."

Epilogue

—•••—

Three weeks later

CATHERINE SAT ON HER PATIO, the afternoon sun beating down around her. She embraced the solitude of her garden, hoping the beauty of the flowers would help to heal her broken heart. She vaguely thought she heard the doorbell ring, but she didn't move. She knew Lucy would tend to whoever was there.

"Miss Catherine," Lucy said softly, "Captain Manny is here for you. Do you want to see him, or should I say you're resting?"

"Lucy, show him in and tell him he'd better bring Peaches with him."

"Yes, Miss Catherine. I'll surely tell him," Lucy said smiling.

Manny was preceded by a very exuberant dog. Peaches rushed over to Catherine and sat in front of her waiting to be caressed. She was rewarded for her patience.

"Cat, it's so good to see you," Manny said, bending to give her a kiss on the cheek.

Lucy bustled out carrying a vase of yellow and white daisies with three spikes of blue irises. "Captain Manny brought these to you. Aren't they pretty?"

"Yes. They're beautiful. Thank you, Lucy, and will you bring us some ice tea with lemon wedges?"

"I certainly will."

"Thank you, Manny, for the flowers." Tears quickly filled her eyes. Catherine pulled a handkerchief from her jeans pocket and wiped the moisture away, but more tears followed. "I'm sorry, Manny, I thought I was done crying. We didn't know each other very long, but the time we had was so very special. Now I can't seem to find the will to face the day, let alone the nights." She folded the damp hanky in her lap.

Lucy brought out a pitcher and set it on the table along with a small plate of sugar cookies. She poured two tall glasses of tea over ice, added the lemon, and then retreated into the house.

"I know what you mean, Cat. Pete cried like a baby when I visited to give him the details about what happened. He feels he should have been there, that somehow he could have helped."

"I was there, and, yet, I couldn't help either," she said wistfully.

"Speaking of helping, you provided a significant link you know," Manny said. "When you saw the picture on my galley table and told me that Ted Adams had an identical tattoo, your information led us in a new direction. Adam's involvement was a key piece of information we lacked. We had two pieces of luck. If the boat hadn't beached during the storm, three-million dollars of coke would have been sold on the street. And then, you recognized the tattoo in the photo that tied Adams to the case."

Manny topped off their glasses of ice tea and popped a fresh lemon wedge into each. "Tell you what, enough of this gloomy talk. Hutch would want you to live your life to the fullest. I'll give you some good news if you'll give me a piece of something upbeat as well. Deal?" he asked.

"Deal," Catherine said, smiling in spite of her heavy heart.

"Pete made a killing on the Triple Crown," Manny said.

"But I heard Big Brown lost. I know he favored him."

"Yes, but the handicapper he followed, Santiago, gave him some terrific background on the other horses in the race. Adding his own savvy twist to the pick, Pete put together several winning combinations. He lost a couple of the bets, but he won big on what Pete described as the exotics. He won $48,000 on what he called a superfecta. He won another $3,700 on an exotic called the trifecta and several hundred on another wager. I lost track of what he was saying at that point."

"My goodness, I guess he did make a killing. What's he going to do with all those winnings? Vacation in Hawaii?"

"No. You'll like this. He's setting up a scholarship fund for law-enforcement students in Hutch's name at the University of Michigan, where Hutch went to school."

"What a wonderful idea. I'll have to call him so I can add to the fund," Catherine said, dabbing at another tear in her eye.

"Hey, now. I didn't mean to make you cry again."

"No no. I'm fine. Believe me...I don't think I can shed many more tears."

"Okay. Now it's your turn. Tell me something good."

"Well," Catherine said with a sigh, willing herself to move forward, "I had a call from Russell Stone this morning. It seems the Pelican Bay Marina investors want to go ahead with the renovation plans I drew up. One of the investors is going to take over the marina, and he wants me to manage the project. Russell hopes I will say yes and meet with the man next week to propose a schedule."

"That sounds like a good idea...going back to the marina."

"Yes, I suppose so. And then, there's the House of Beads expansion. In fact, I'm due to meet with Tillie and Pete in the morning. Pete agreed to sign on in a consulting capacity, if we go ahead with the cyber café idea. I promised Tillie I would put up the venture capital. The rough designs are finished. We still have to pull together the cost analysis. That's where Pete comes in. That, and how to make the network perform efficiently."

Manny saw Catherine's mood swing up a bit as she replaced her thoughts of Hutch, at least for a few minutes, with the love of her work—especially the two new projects.

"Cat, that's terrific news. I think that calls for a celebration. Would you have dinner with an old bachelor and his pooch tomorrow night? You can fill me in on this cyber café and how all the pieces are going to fit together."

"Dinner with you and Peaches would be nice."

At the sound of her name, Peaches leaned in closer to Catherine, giving her arm a nudge and her hand a soft tender kiss.

The End

REVIEW REQUEST

Dear reader, I hope you enjoyed meeting a new friend, Elizabeth Stitchway. If you have the time, it would mean a lot to me if you wrote a review, your honest appraisal. What did you like most? It's super easy.

Go to Amazon. Log in. Search: <u>Mary Jane Forbes Intercept</u>

Thank you!

House of Beads Mystery Series

Murder in the House of Beads, A Mystery in Paradise
Intercept, A Treacherous Race to the Triple Crown
Checkmate, a Deadly Game of Cyber Espionage
Identity Theft, Terrorists are on the Prowl

Book 3 in the House of Beads Mystery Series

— • • • —

— ● ● ● —

SUMMARY

A cyber breach worth millions. A conspiracy that could take down a city. A detective and an IT expert may be the city's only hope…

Brenda Kittles is excited for her new start as a computer security expert for a prestigious Daytona Beach architectural firm. But her anxiety builds when an explosion and a dead body point to a cyber crime on her watch. Eager to please her new boss Catherine Hainsworth, she shares the evidence with the city's hardest working police captain.

Manny Salinas is just moving on from Catherine when the cyber breach sends him right back to her. Doing his best to put his old flame out of his mind, he and Brenda realize the chess-obsessed hacker may want to play a game with millions of dollars. With the help of his second in command, the captain and the rookie computer expert must track the criminal across Europe to keep Catherine's company alive.

Can Brenda and Manny save the firm from collapse or will the devious cyber thief send Daytona Beach reeling?

Checkmate is the third standalone book in the intriguing House of Beads romantic suspense series. If you like interwoven plots, colorful local characters, and a dash of romance, then you'll love Mary Jane Forbes' clever page-turner.

Buy *Checkmate* to solve a cyber-mystery today!

Books by Mary Jane Forbes

FICTION

Bradley Farm Series
Bradley Farm, Sadie, Finn
Jeli, Marshall, Georgie

Twists of Fate Series
The Fisherman, a love story
The Witness, living a lie
Twists of Fate, daring to dream

Murder by Design, Series:
Murder by Design
Labeled in Seattle
Choices, And the Courage to Risk

Elizabeth Stitchway, PI, Series
The Mailbox, Black Magic,
The Painter, Twister

House of Beads Mystery Series
Murder in the House of Beads
Intercept, Checkmate
Identity Theft

Novels
The Baby Quilt ... a mystery!
The Message...Call Me!

Short Stories
Once Upon a Christmas Eve, a Romantic Fairy Tale
The Christmas Angel and the Magic Holiday Tree

Visit: www.MaryJaneForbes.com

Aqua Treasure
Necklace Pattern

Pendant

- 3 center-drilled transparent, faceted Aqua colored teardrops, 13x18mm
- 4 6mm indicolite bicones, CSE*
- 3 4mm indicolite bicones from CSE
- 1" (four links) 5mm hammered cable chain
- 3 4mm silver daisy spacers
- 7 22ga. Head pins

Necklace

- 10 16mm faceted, transparent aqua colored glass square beads
- 8 matte aqua barbell-shaped glass beads, about 10mm long
- 16 4mm indicolite colored bicones, CSE
- 2 6mm indicolite colored bicones, CSE
- 20 4mm silver daisy spacers
- 18 10mm long twisted silver bugle beads
- 21 inches of Soft Touch beading wire, .019 diameter
- 1 silver lobster claw clasp
- 1 6mm closed jump ring
- 2 silver 2x2mm crimps
- 2 3mm crimp covers

*Crystallized Swarovski Elements®

Aqua Treasure jewelry Catherine wore to the Chamber of Commerce Charity Auction

Courtesy of Imagine That!®

Directions

Pendant

To make this pendant, dangle the beads from the length of cable chain.

1. On first head pin, place a 4mm indicolite colored bicone, a daisy spacer and the aqua colored teardrop.
2. Make a wire-wrapped loop connecting the head pin to the bottom link of chain.
3. Take a second head pin. Place a 6mm indicolite bicone on the pin.
4. Make a wire-wrapped loop connecting the head pin also to the last link of chain.
5. On a third head pin, place a 4mm crystal, a 4mm daisy spacer, and an aqua teardrop.
6. Make a wire-wrapped loop connecting the head pin to the second-to-last link of chain.
7. On another head pin, put a 6mm crystal and make a wire-wrapped loop to connect that head pin to the second-to-last link of chain.
8. Repeat steps 5-7 to add a teardrop and 6mm crystal to the third-to-last link of chain.
9. On the last head pin, place a 6mm indicolite crystal and wire-wrap the head pin to the top link of chain. Set aside.

Necklace

1. Attach the closed jump ring by adding a crimp bead, looping your beading wire through the ring and back through the crimp. Make sure to leave as long a piece of wire to string on as possible. Fold the crimp and add crimp cover.
2. Now, string the beads in the following pattern until you have five of the 16mm aqua glass squares on your beading wire:
   a) A 4mm silver daisy spacer, one 16mm aqua glass square, 4mm daisy spacer, a silver bugle bead, a 4mm indicolite bicone crystal, a barbell bead, a 4mm indicolite bicone crystal, a silver bugle bead. Repeat.
3. Once you have the fifth glass square bead strung, add a 4mm daisy spacer, a silver bugle bead, a 4mm daisy spacer, and one 6mm indicolite bicone crystal.
4. String the beading wire through the top link of the pendant chain.
5. Now string another 6mm indicolite bicone crystal, a 4mm daisy spacer, a silver bugle bead, a 4mm silver daisy spacer and a 16mm aqua glass square.
6. Continue until all five of the 16mm aqua squares are strung.
7. Attach clasp—add a crimp bead, string beading wire through clasp and back through the crimp.
8. Fold the crimp and add crimp cover.

www.ingramcontent.com/pod-product-compliance
Lightning Source LLC
Chambersburg PA
CBHW070831120626
46556CB00002B/721